# THIS IS HOW I ROLL

## DEBBI MICHIKO FLORENCE

SCHOLASTIC INC.

Text copyright © 2023 by Debbi Michiko Florence

ISBN 978-1-338-78556-2

10 9 8 7 6 5 4 3 2 1       23 24 25 26 27

Printed in the U.S.A.     40
First printing 2023

Book design by Stephanie Yang

To my soul sister, Andrea Wang, who shares my love for sushi, xiao long bao, and boba tea!

Also by Debbi Michiko Florence

*Keep It Together, Keiko Carter*

*Just Be Cool, Jenna Sakai*

*Sweet and Sour*

# 1

If there's one thing I've learned from my dad, it's that following your dreams is important. Not that he's ever said as much to me. Dad is not the talkative type. In fact, neither of my parents is and that's okay, because actions speak louder than words. And before this summer is over, my actions will prove to my dad that I am worth having in his restaurant kitchen and ready to be taught how to cook great Japanese food.

Which was why I was in our home kitchen earlier than I normally ever woke up, especially on the first weekend of summer.

"Where is it?" I asked out loud even though I was alone. I was determined to make the perfect breakfast.

This setup was not nearly as nice as the one we'd had in San Francisco. I missed our bright and airy kitchen with white subway tiles and stainless-steel appliances. This one was definitely dated, with apricot countertops and dark-wood cabinets.

I flung open the island's cabinet door and yanked out every single pot and pan, tossing them onto the counter to join all the lids I'd already grabbed. Then I slid on sock feet to the shelves next to our basic white oven, pulling out baking sheets and muffin pans. But as I reached toward the cabinet next to the sink, my hand knocked into the tower of pot lids and they all came crashing down onto the floor. I would have cringed, but the lids were an improvement over the vinyl floor with its mint-green squares.

"Goodness, Sana, sweetie. What are you doing?"

I spun around to face my mom, who was dressed for her morning run in black shorts and a neon-orange tank top, her shiny black hair in a high ponytail. It still took getting used to, not only having Mom at home more often, but seeing her in running clothes instead of her business skirts and blazers. When we lived in San Francisco, the only kind of running she did was out the door to her job every morning.

"Hey, Mom," I said with a sheepish wave.

"Good thing your father is already at the restaurant. You could wake the dead with the racket you're making."

I, of course, knew Dad had left an hour ago. Although there

was no rule against me cooking, Dad wasn't a fan of me messing around in his kitchen.

"Your cousin will be here in five minutes," Mom said. "What are you looking for?"

I contemplated my answer to Mom's seemingly simple question. The thing was, communication in my family was complicated. Sometimes a twist of the truth was easier. The less said, the less anyone would worry. My parents were all about protecting me, even though I'd rather know what was going on.

Case in point: Most of what I knew about Piper Bay and my parents' decision to move here I'd learned from my cousin, Charli. Her dad, my uncle Luke, owned a successful real estate company and had helped Dad find the perfect place for his sushi restaurant. My parents hadn't ever really asked me what I thought about leaving. And before I knew it, we were living two hours south of San Francisco in a small, pretty town no one had barely ever heard of before. Fortunately, I made friends easily, so starting a new school in the seventh grade hadn't freaked me out. Plus I had Charli here. She wasn't just a cousin, she was also my best friend. So even though my parents had kind of left me in the dark about the move, Charli had told me everything she'd heard. She knew I liked to have all the facts.

This morning I opted for the whole truth. "Where's the tamago pan?" I asked.

"If you want a Japanese omelet, why don't you just ask Dad to make it when he gets home?"

I sighed. That was the problem. "Mom, I want to make tamago on my own. Dad would just chase me out of the kitchen anyway." He had a lot of rules both in his restaurant and at home. Besides, I wanted to make the homestyle rolled tamago, while Dad undoubtedly would make his high-end fancy sushi-style custardy tamago.

"Oh, Sana, your father wouldn't keep you out of the kitchen," Mom said. Of course she took Dad's side.

"Yo, what's up?" Charli called, kicking off her shoes before darting into the house. "Whoa. What a mess! Is Uncle Hiro home?"

She knew as well as I did that he'd hit the roof if he saw his pristine kitchen like this.

"Take a guess," I said. "Hi, Uncle Luke!"

"Happy Sunday, Sana." Uncle Luke's smile was the exact

same as Mom's, quirking a little higher on the left side. He stayed at the back door so he wouldn't have to take his shoes off.

"Let's go!" Mom quickly put on her running shoes.

"And they're off," I said as the door slammed.

"Ugh." Charli slumped on a kitchen chair. Her chestnut-brown pixie cut stuck up like porcupine quills. "It's finally summer. I wanted to sleep in. Our families get up way too early."

I threw open another cabinet. "Help me look for the tamago pan."

"What's it look like?" Charli stayed put at the table, not even making a show of helping me.

"It's a stainless-steel rectangle with a wooden handle."

"And *tamago* is *egg*, right?"

Charli didn't speak Japanese. I didn't either, really, but I understood a little because my parents spoke it once in a while, mostly when they were upset or wanted to say things they didn't want me to know. Plus I'd made it a point to learn food-related words in Japanese.

"Yes. Come help me!" I stood on my toes to try to see behind the plates. Not that I thought the pan might be back there. Dad was very organized and pans didn't go with plates.

"Um, hi, Uncle Hiro," Charli chirped.

"Ha ha," I said, without turning around. "Don't try to scare me. Dad's at the restaurant already."

"Susannah!"

I yelped and spun around, knocking two baking sheets to the ground to join the pot lids I hadn't yet picked up.

"Hi, Daddy."

He frowned as he took in the disaster of his kitchen. "Don't 'hi, Daddy' me. Why does my kitchen look like this?"

"What are you doing here?" I asked.

Charli, who was no help, made her way silently upstairs to my bedroom.

"I live here," he said, grinning and lifting an amused eyebrow.

"Funny, Dad." I started to pick up the lids off the floor and stick them back into the cabinet.

"Ah! Dameda!"

I nearly dropped everything again. "What's wrong?"

"You can't just put them back in the cabinet! They were on the floor! You need to wash them."

I glanced down at the huge pile of lids. "No! Dad! The floor is so clean you can eat off it." Dad swept and mopped the kitchen before he went to bed every night.

He flapped his hand at me. I sighed. Foiled once again by the Mikami Way. I piled the lids into the sink. It was going to be a while before I could join Charli upstairs. Not that she would care—she was probably already on my laptop watching crafting videos.

Dad opened the fridge and pulled out stacked containers, which he placed in the soft-sided cooler he'd brought with him.

"So, seriously, why are you home?" I stuck the plug into the drain and turned on the water, squirting dish soap into the sink. Maybe Dad would leave before I had to wash *all* the lids.

"The crew is running late, so I came home to grab some more fresh ingredients."

The crew was the film crew. A director had contacted Dad in the spring, wanting to do a short documentary on him. Mikami Sushi had been a finalist for Best New Restaurant in California and then been featured in several articles in food and travel magazines. I had been excited to learn that the filmmaker was none other than Baxton Ferguson. He had won an award two years ago for a documentary he'd done on sustainably caught fish that Dad and I had watched together. Not that Dad had much time to sit around and watch movies with me anymore.

Since opening over a year ago, Dad's ten-seat sushi bar had become so popular, people came from all over just to try his food. Weekend reservations for his omakase Chef's Choice dinner menu were booked weeks in advance. It was no wonder Baxton was interested. And after a couple of weeks of phone interviews, he and his crew arrived last week to start filming.

"Can I come watch?"

My heart sunk as Dad shook his head. "It's summer. Go have fun." When I didn't respond, Dad asked, "Don't you and Charli have plans?"

That was Dad's way of discouraging me. He never outright said no, but after twelve years, I knew how to read between the lines and fill in the blanks on my own.

Dad zipped up the cooler and looked around the kitchen again, wincing like it physically pained him to see the mess. "What were you looking for anyway?"

"Tamago pan," I said, not having the energy to deflect.

"Why didn't you say you wanted tamago?" Dad grinned and

ruffled my hair. He reached up to the cabinet over the fridge, the one place I hadn't looked because I'd need a step stool to get up there.

"Can I help?" I asked.

"I've got this." He nodded to the sink.

So while I washed the lids that didn't really need washing, Dad made tamago, even though the only reason I'd been looking for the pan was to try making it myself. I'd asked him to teach me countless times, but he always had a dried-out excuse ready to serve me.

By the time I finished cleaning up, Dad had made two gorgeous rolled Japanese omelets, plated on blue-and-white dishes with a garnish of green onions cut on the bias. He set the table with chopsticks laid on origami crane holders.

"Charli!" Dad called up the stairs. "Come eat!"

I dried my hands and joined Charli at the table. She loved my dad's cooking. Everyone did, including me, of course, but more than anything I wanted to be a successful chef like him, even if he did everything he could to stop me.

# 2

After Dad left, Charli and I finished eating and headed upstairs. My loft was the only room on the second floor, and I loved it, even if it didn't have a door. The house, a super cute pink cottage, was a rental that needed work, as Uncle Luke had said when he'd found it for us. When Dad left his job at a popular sushi restaurant in San Francisco to follow his dream of opening his own place, he'd put our home, the one he'd grown up in, on the market. Uncle Luke said Dad made a killing. All the money went into Dad's restaurant. At least that's what Charli told me.

The reduced rent on this place included the deal that my parents would fix up the cottage. Good luck with that since neither of them was very handy. Mom had spent my entire childhood at a high-powered sales and marketing job at a hotel chain. Now she worked part-time at a boutique hotel in nearby Carmel.

I sat on the floor where Charli had dumped her big bag of craft supplies.

"So, what are we doing today?"

I happily joined Charli whenever she tried a new craft or art technique, which was pretty much all the time. I wasn't horrible at it, but everything Charli did looked amazing.

"Mosaics." Charli opened her laptop and hit play so I could see the process. She loved watching both art and crafting how-to videos. There were a couple she subscribed to and followed religiously.

This current project looked easy enough, though I knew Charli's would be museum worthy. I sketched out a sushi roll on paper while Charli started tearing up pieces of colored tissue paper.

"I wish I could figure out what my thing was," Charli said, making piles for different hues.

"Your thing is art," I said, erasing a crooked line. Charli was great at all art. I wasn't bad, but it was definitely her thing, like cooking was mine.

"But I want to focus on one specific medium. Whatever that is," Charli sighed. "If only I'd gotten into that summer program."

The Pasadena Art Institute ran a special summer program for gifted students ages twelve and up. Charli had learned about it four years ago and had been counting down until she could apply. She had been crushed when she hadn't gotten in.

"You can apply again next year," I said. "And didn't you say you were at the top of the wait list?"

"Yeah, but who would drop out? It's hard enough to get into as is." Charli pulled her sketch pad onto her lap. Her pencil moved across it, and like magic an image of a monarch butterfly in a field appeared.

"Well, at least we have each other this summer." I grinned at her.

Charli smiled back at me. "And we will work our way through every crafting video on the internet!"

I kept the grin on my face, hoping it didn't falter into a grimace. Don't get me wrong: I loved hanging out with Charli and doing crafts with her, but sometimes I wished we could mix it up and cook instead. But Charli was a disaster in the kitchen. Last summer, our first one together in Piper Bay, she'd burned toast so badly she'd started a very small fire in the toaster. We'd put it out immediately, but that ended Charli ever wanting to cook again.

My phone chimed with a group text from my San Francisco friends, and I put down my pencil to check in.

**Alana:**
Girl, where are you? It's summer! Talk to us!

**Liv:**
Sana has abandoned us.

**Esme:**
She doesn't love us anymore.

**Sana:**
You all are sooooo hilarious.

**Esme:**
She speaks! She's alive!

**Sana:**
Happy summer!

**Liv:**
I miss you! Esme and Alana are busy
with their boyfriends, so I'm all alone.

**Alana:**
Hey! That's not true! I spend
tons of time with you.

**Esme:**

Summer romance! I'm in heaven.


**Liv:**

Seriously, Sana, come back. I
get to listen to this 24/7.


**Alana:**

Maybe Sana has a boyfriend?
Anything you want to share with us?
A crush?

---

**Sana:**

Nothing. And I miss you all, too.
Hope we can get together a few times this summer.


**Liv:**

For sure!


I didn't want to be rude to Charli, so I texted that I'd catch
them later. Charli had already started on her mosaic. I joined in
as I relayed the text thread to her. She'd met my friends a few
times when she used to visit me in San Francisco.

"Boyfriends? Really?" she asked.

I shrugged. I wasn't against the idea of a boyfriend, but there
wasn't anyone I was even mildly interested in. Honestly, the only

thing I cared about was becoming the best cook possible. I loved the feeling of mixing ingredients together and ending up with something delicious to share. It made me feel accomplished. And I really wanted that connection with Dad. He loved cooking. I did, too.

As I tore pieces of black tissue paper for the nori in my sushi roll, I realized I had to come up with a strong game plan to prove to my dad he should teach me to cook again. It had been two years since that last time. I was determined to change his mind and I didn't want to waste the summer.

# 3

The next morning, I woke up early again, changed out of my pajamas, and scooted down the stairs to the kitchen, feeling light and happy. The restaurant was closed on Mondays and Tuesdays, but let's face it, since Dad opened Mikami Sushi, he was rarely ever home. Even on his days off he planned and prepped and cleaned and created. There was only one exception. When we moved to Piper Bay, Mondays had become family breakfast days.

Mom walked into the quiet kitchen still in her bathrobe.

"Where's Dad?" I asked.

"The film crew wanted to take advantage of the empty restaurant and do some filming and interviewing."

"But what about breakfast?"

"I'll make it."

That gave me an idea. "No! Let me!"

Mom raised her eyebrows. "You sure?"

"Yes!" I already knew what I wanted to try. I'd found a video of a Japanese American home cook who shared her recipes. Her Japanese fluffy pancakes totally caught my eye, and while the recipe seemed challenging, it looked doable. I'd already watched the video three times the day before while Charli was writing up a long art supply shopping list for the rest of our summer. "Go for your run," I told my mom. "I'll have breakfast ready by the time you get back."

"That's nice, Sana. Thanks."

A great thing about having a chef for a dad was that we had a fully stocked pantry and fridge. I pulled out all the ingredients and starting prepping. Dad had taught me to have all my ingredients measured and ready before starting to cook. It meant more dishes to wash, but it was the Mikami Way, and things were *always* done the Mikami Way in this house and in his restaurant.

I separated eggs, mixed the ingredients, and finally, heated the nonstick pan. The first two pancakes were raw in the middle because I had the burner too high, so I adjusted the flame and by the second batch, I made perfectly fluffy soufflé pancakes. Getting them just right had me feeling as fizzy and light as the pancakes themselves.

Whenever I was chopping and measuring, I felt calm and in control. Recipes were guidelines and there was something very reassuring about knowing what to expect and how my work should turn out. But I also had fun when I got to experiment and put my own spin on things. Being in charge *and* making things up was a blast. This is what I wanted to do. This is what I *loved* to do.

By the time Mom got home, I had breakfast warming in the oven, the table set, and her coffee and my orange juice poured. When she sat down, I presented her with three fluffy pancakes dusted with powdered sugar and served with fresh berries.

"Oh, Sana! This looks amazing!" she exclaimed as I joined her with my own plate.

My pancakes were less uniform, but when I cut into them, they were fully steam cooked inside. Whew.

We ate quickly, the only sounds our quiet chewing and our forks scraping across our plates. Mom sighed as she finished. "Those were the best pancakes I've ever had in my life."

I gobbled up my last bite and flashed Mom a grin. "Really? Better than the pancakes you ate in Japan?"

"If not better, just as good."

Mom and Dad had met in Japan. Dad had moved there after high school and ended up working in restaurants for over a decade. It was where he'd learned to be a sushi chef. Mom had gone on vacation to Japan a couple of years after she graduated from college and they'd randomly met when she ate at the restaurant where he worked. They hit it off, he'd asked her out, and they'd spent the entire week together. When Mom went back to the States after her vacation, they'd kept in touch, and she was the reason he moved back to California less than a year later. Six months after that, they got married. I loved this story. It was rare that my parents shared their personal history with me, so I held this one close to my heart.

"I'll do the breakfast dishes," Mom said after we finished eating. I'd already done all the cleanup from cooking. It was the Mikami Way to clean as you went.

I carried my dishes to the sink and then took out a plate of three pancakes from the still-warm oven. When Mom raised her eyebrows and made yummy sounds, I laughed and backed away from her.

"Is that for Charli?" she asked.

"Nope. It's for Dad."

"Oh, Sana, I don't have time to take you over to the restaurant. I'm meeting a friend of Uncle Luke's who is an interior designer. Do you want to come?"

"On your friend date?" I shook my head.

Mom laughed, sounding like tinkling bells. "No, I'm picking her brain for ideas on how to renovate and redecorate this house. It's part of our rental deal, remember?"

I remembered. It was just surprising that Mom was interested in fixing up the house.

"It's okay," I said. "I'm riding my bike to Charli's anyway." The great thing about Piper Bay was that it was a small town. I had never been allowed to go anywhere by myself in San Francisco. Here, I was allowed to ride my bike to Charli's and other nearby locations like Dad's restaurant, as long as I checked in with Mom or Dad when I left and when I arrived there. There were a lot of rules, but I followed them, which was why they trusted me.

"Dad's very busy and distracted. You know the film crew is shooting today."

"I'm just going to drop breakfast off and then go to Charli's," I said. "I won't bother him or get in the way." Though what I really hoped was that when Dad saw me and the awesome pancakes I'd made, he would invite me to cook with him or at least hang out while they filmed the documentary.

Ever since I was a little kid, Dad had taught me kitchen safety. By the time I was eight, I was chopping vegetables with a real knife on my own. And soon after I was making side dishes without his help. I'd felt like a real sous-chef.

One night when I was ten, Dad came home from work. Mom had already put me to bed, but I snuck out into the hallway to listen because my parents only talked about interesting things when they thought I was asleep.

A woman had applied for an open position as a sushi chef. Dad's boss said that women couldn't make sushi. Something about their body temperature being too high? Whatever. He wouldn't even look at the application. I had been so angry that he hadn't even interviewed the woman, because someday that might be me. I wondered then if Dad had felt the same. That women shouldn't be sushi chefs. It wasn't something I could ever ask him because I wasn't supposed to be listening in the first place.

A couple of days later, when Dad was teaching me how to

make Japanese curry from scratch, I had accidentally put sugar instead of flour into the roux. I'd been singing along to the music playing and hadn't been paying attention. To be fair, Mom had moved the canisters and had put the sugar in front of the flour. Mom didn't follow the rules in our kitchen as closely as I did. But all the same, I should have noticed. Dad had snapped at me and I'd cried. All lessons stopped and not long after, we moved to Piper Bay. Dad wouldn't teach me or let me hang out at his restaurant either.

But I was going to change his mind by cooking something so spectacular, he'd not only be impressed, I would win his respect. Then he'd see how serious I was and maybe, just maybe, he'd show me how to cook again and even allow me to work in his restaurant. And it had to happen soon. Once summer was over and school was back in session, my studies would be the priority. Mom always made that clear.

The pancakes I made this morning would need to prove to Dad that I was worthy.

# 4

When I pulled up to Mikami Sushi, there was a big truck, an unfamiliar car, plus Dad's little Honda, parked in the small lot behind the restaurant. I locked my bike to the lamppost near the back door and removed the wrapped package of pancakes from the wire basket.

The tiny kitchen was empty and, not surprisingly, sparkling clean.

As I walked through the cloth noren separating the kitchen from the dining area, I spotted studio lights and reflector screens set up around the restaurant, along with a camera facing the sushi bar, where my dad stood. A man wearing a bright yellow T-shirt sat at the bar across from Dad, notepad in his hand. All activity stopped when everyone noticed me.

"Um, hi, Dad." I felt my cheeks turn pink, like I'd walked onto a stage, which I guess I had.

"Susannah, what are you doing here?"

My face flushed even hotter, realizing that the film crew was witnessing his displeasure at my appearance.

"Um, I brought you pancakes." I lifted the cloth-wrapped package.

"Is your daughter a chef in the making?" The man in the yellow shirt had to be Baxton Ferguson. "You must be proud to have a family member to hand the business down to."

Dad scowled, his thick eyebrows meeting in the middle of his forehead.

It only took that look to break my heart. Again.

"Excuse us a moment," Dad said to the man.

I knew he was going to have a private talk with me in the kitchen. Before that happened, I leaned over the counter and put out my hand. "Hi! I'm Sana."

Yellow-shirt man smiled as he shook it. "Baxton Ferguson." He nodded behind him to the camera person. "That's Shelby." And then to the man holding a reflector shield. "And my brother Griff. He helps out during filming and also edits the footage."

"It's great to meet you," I said. "We loved your documentary on sustainable fish."

He raised his eyebrows. "A young fan! Excellent!"

Dad took the package from me, and I reluctantly followed him into the kitchen.

"Thank you, Susannah." He kept his voice low because there was no door between the kitchen and the tiny sushi bar.

"I made them fluffy Japanese style. Mom loved them," I said, a little too eagerly.

"Okay."

"Are you going to try them?"

Dad removed his white sushi chef's cap and ran his hand through his salt-and-pepper hair, though since he opened his restaurant, it was looking more salt than pepper. "I will. Later." He placed the cloth-wrapped package on the counter. "Are you headed to Charli's, then?"

"In a bit." I hoped to hang around and watch the filming.

"Now," he said. He was always trying to keep me far away from his kitchen.

"Why can't I stay?"

"Go do some of those fun projects you and Charli always do," Dad said firmly. "That's what summers are for."

"Okay," I said, trying not to show my disappointment. I

slipped out the back door. Maybe he would taste my pancakes before he got back to filming. I hung around just in case he wanted to run after me to rave about how perfect they were. But ten minutes later I knew that wasn't going to happen. I sighed and unlocked my bike, then rolled it to the front of the restaurant and climbed on.

Just as I was about to head off, a blue pickup with the words EARTH-LOVE LANDSCAPING on the side pulled up to the curb. Dad had hired a landscaping company in the spring, and the front of the restaurant looked much better than when he first bought the place. A new Japanese maple shaded the walkway. Much of the grass had been removed to make a pretty Zen garden with white rocks. And the bushes by the front door that used to be unruly were now shaped into puffy balls.

A white man stepped out of the truck's driver's side and an Asian boy my age climbed down from the passenger side. My heart stuttered weirdly in my chest. I may have gasped a little. He was very cute, with hair that fell into his eyes, and wore an orange baseball cap with the words EARTH-LOVE LANDSCAP-ING embroidered in green over a picture of the earth. His gray

T-shirt had a matching logo, the short sleeves rolled tightly to his shoulders, which showed off his toned arms.

He walked to the back of the truck, opened the tailgate, and hopped into the bed easily. After he set up a ramp, he rolled down a push mower.

"Hi," I blurted as he guided the mower across the sidewalk in front of me. I didn't want to miss the chance to meet this boy. Charli called the way I made friends easily my superpower.

The boy stopped, blocking my path, and grinned at me. He had a dimple in his left cheek, and was a little taller than me, but not by much.

"Hey," he said back. "You work here?" He nodded at the restaurant.

"I wish. I'd never get hired." There was no way I was going to let him know this was my dad's restaurant. When a few of my classmates found out my dad owned Mikami Sushi, their parents pressed them to see if I could get them a reservation. As if I had that kind of power. If that were true, I'd be working in his restaurant, even if it was washing dishes. I just wanted to be there soaking it all up.

A look I couldn't identify crossed his face, but was gone in an instant. He nodded like he agreed. Well, that was a little rude, but I quickly forgave him because, did I mention, he was very cute?

There were a lot of differences between Piper Bay and San Francisco, and one notable one was the lack of Asians, particularly cute Asian boys. I wanted this boy to know me as me, not the daughter of a popular sushi chef.

A Prius with the same earth logo parked behind the truck. A Latino man stepped out of the car.

Cute Asian Boy called out, "Good morning, Mr. Perez."

Mr. Perez waved and walked to the back of the pickup.

The white man that C.A.B. had shown up with stalked over. "Get started with weeding the beds," he said gruffly.

C.A.B.'s face turned stony. That hard, determined stare only lasted for the briefest second, but it made my heart flutter all the same. I wasn't sure if I was nervous about his bad-boy look or excited. I didn't think bad boys were my type, but having never had a boyfriend or even a serious crush, I had no clue if I even had a type.

C.A.B. turned back to me and said, "I'd better get to work." He smiled. "I'm Koji."

"Sana," I said.

"Tomorrow I'll be working at the library, you know, doing the landscaping there."

"Nice. Maybe I'll see you there."

"That would be cool."

"Koji," Mr. Perez said with a teasing lilt as he walked past us. "Stop flirting."

My cheeks flushed and I expected Koji to turn stony again, but instead he smiled at Mr. Perez and saluted. Then he waved to me as he walked over to the front of the restaurant.

I grinned all the way to Charli's.

# 5

The first thing I did when I got to my cousin's house was tell her about Cute Asian Boy and his landscaping job.

"And he's working at the library tomorrow," I said.

"I guess we're going to the library," Charli said with a grin.

I felt all fizzy and warm thinking of seeing Koji again.

"What's the name of the landscaping company?" she asked, opening her laptop. "We need to see if they're legit."

I rolled my eyes. Charli was the overprotective type. When I started seventh grade at her school last year, she walked me to each of my classes the first week even though I insisted I was fine on my own. She worried over me more than my own parents did. It was nice in a way, but sometimes her concern felt stifling. I didn't like being told what I could or could not do. I got enough of that from my dad.

But it was easier to give in than to fight her. "Earth-Love Landscaping," I said.

Charli raised her eyebrows and closed her laptop.

"What?"

"They're legit."

"How do you know?"

"Because they were on the local news. They're an environmentally friendly business. No gas mowers or leaf blowers, and they encourage their clients to use drought-resistant plants and stuff. They won some kind of award for new, small, green businesses or something."

"Wow. You know a lot about landscaping companies."

"Ha! No. I just remember them because my dad hired them to work on curb appeal for listings. That's probably how your dad heard about them."

Charli and her dad were close. Her mom had died of cancer when she was five, so Uncle Luke made sure he was there for Charli, supporting and encouraging her. They had Thursday movie nights and inside jokes, laughed a lot, and were basically best friends. Sometimes I was jealous of their closeness. Not that

I wanted to be best friends with my parents, but I wished they would talk to me about things.

"What are we doing today?" I nodded to the paintbrushes and two plastic palettes on the kitchen table.

"Watercolor washes," Charli said as she handed me some paper. Then she opened her laptop back up and showed me the how-to video.

I appreciated that she included me, but sometimes I wouldn't have minded a break. "You know, you can just do the projects you want to do. I can entertain myself."

"I want to do things *with* you. It's more fun this way." Charli handed me a paintbrush. "So, this cute boy. You said he's Asian? Not a lot of those in Piper Bay."

"I know, right? And he's Japanese!"

Charli gave me the side-eye. "It's not true that you can tell from looking at someone."

"No duh!" I rolled my eyes. "He told me his name and it's Japanese."

"Oh! What is it?"

"Koji."

Charli stared at me. "Koji?" she repeated.

I didn't like the look on Charli's face. It was her *danger danger* look—the one she got when I was using the stove or a sharp knife.

"That's an unusual name." Charli shook her head. "I went to elementary school with a Koji."

"And?"

"He was a troublemaker."

"How can someone be a troublemaker in elementary school? Like what? He didn't raise his hand or line up properly?"

Charli made a face at me. "No, I mean like he'd act up."

"How?"

"Sana!"

"What? Don't get all frustrated with me. Just tell me what made him a troublemaker." Charli had a tendency to overreact and judge.

"He got expelled at the end of fifth grade."

That got my attention. "How does someone get expelled from elementary school?"

"He punched someone."

I gasped. "Did you see it happen?"

"No, but I was friends with the boy Koji punched."

"Why did he punch him?"

Charli shot me a look. "Does it matter?"

She wasn't wrong. Punching another person was bad.

"He had issues," Charli said. "Like he wouldn't listen to our teacher, Mr. Gibs. And he got into a lot of arguments with other kids."

Charli and I stared at each other as I ran through worst-case scenarios: Koji came from a loan shark family, and the other kid's parents were behind on payments so Koji was sending a message. Or Koji's parents and the other kid's parents were rivals, which meant Koji and the boy were at war. I shook my head, clearing it of silly stories.

"Guys get into fights sometimes, right?" I asked.

"That doesn't make it okay. He got expelled, Sana," Charli said. "And then he disappeared."

"What do you mean, disappeared? I saw him this morning."

"I mean, I heard he got sent to LA that summer. Maybe to a juvenile delinquent facility."

My heart deflated like a bad soufflé. "Is that a fact or are you making things up?"

"It's a good guess."

I didn't want to believe that Koji was dangerous or a bad influence. He seemed so nice. I pushed the memory of his brief scowl out of my head. "You don't know for sure. And if he's back, then that must mean he's better. All rehabilitated or something. Let's not make assumptions. Innocent until proven guilty."

I was good at filling in the blanks, and I chose to fill in this blank with a good story. Koji was misunderstood. That or the teacher had it out for him.

Charli frowned. "Well, he doesn't go to our school. Unless he just got back, but then where has he been all this time? My jail theory works."

"Oh, just come with me to the library tomorrow. You can see if it's the same boy at least," I said.

"Don't forget you're trying to get your dad to teach you to cook again." Charli opened her set of watercolors and dipped her brush into water. "Boys will only distract you."

I wasn't going to get distracted. But there was also nothing wrong with wanting to get to know someone new. Koji's smile, his toned arms, his warm brown eyes, flitted through my mind. As we worked on our watercolor washes, I hoped against hope that there were two Kojis in Piper Bay and that Charli's bad-boy Koji was not the same as mine.

# 6

The next morning, when Charli and I rode our bikes to the library, the landscaping truck was already parked in the lot. Mr. Perez was trimming the bushes in front. He nodded to me, grinned, and pointed to the side of the building. I felt my cheeks flush.

"I guess we're totally obvious," I mumbled as I led Charli around the building.

She laughed. "So what?"

We rounded the corner to find Koji watering the flower beds. He wore a tank contraption strapped to his back and, as before, he'd rolled his short sleeves to his shoulders, showing off his arms. As he watered, he smiled. And that made me smile. Despite his scowl the other day, it seemed like he really did love gardening. Anyone with a passion was okay by me.

Koji turned and when our eyes caught, I squeaked. He waved

and started to walk toward us. My heart sizzled like pork belly on a grill.

"That's definitely him," Charli whispered. As Koji stopped in front of us, Charli grabbed my arm and took a step back.

He raised his eyebrows at her. But I wasn't going to let her paranoia sway me. He seemed perfectly nice, and he had a summer job with a reputable company. I chose to believe the story in my head instead of Charli's less flattering one.

"Hey," I said. "This is my cousin, Charli."

Koji turned his smile on her. "Hi!" When Charli didn't respond, he cocked his head, studying her. "Do I know you?" he asked.

"Yeah. Otter Elementary."

"Oh, yeah. Charlotte Hirai."

"Charli," she corrected him with an edge in her voice.

I gently shook my arm free of her grip and grinned at Koji, trying to make up for Charli's brusqueness.

"Okay, everyone, break time is over," called Mr. Perez as he came around the corner. "Koji'll be done around noon."

"We have plans," Charli jumped in.

I shot her a look.

"That's too bad. Do you want to trade numbers?" Koji asked. "Maybe we can get together another time."

Before Charli could stop me, I whipped my phone out, unlocked it, and handed it to Koji, who entered his number. When he handed my phone back, he said, "Now text me so I have your number."

I promptly typed "hey this is Sana" and his phone buzzed. "Great!" he said. "I'll message you later!"

Charli grabbed my arm and nearly dragged me back to our bikes.

"You're being totally rude," I whispered as we unlocked them.

"That boy is trouble, Sana."

"You don't know that! All you know is that he moved away and now he's back."

"I know for a fact he was expelled. For fighting," Charli huffed. "And he's too young to have a job. That means he's probably working because he has to. Maybe the courts forced him—like probation or something."

We rode our bikes in silence back to my house, which wasn't entirely unusual, but I could feel the weight of it on me.

When we got to my room, I sat on my bed, and she leaned

against my desk. "Don't be mad at me," she said. "I'm only looking out for you."

"I don't need you to do that. I need you to be on my side. He's cute. It's not like I'm going to run away and marry him or anything!"

Charli waved her hand. "We have more important things to focus on than boys. Koji isn't going to help you impress your dad with your mad cooking skills."

I sighed. She was right. I didn't know why I was arguing with Charli. It wasn't like I wanted a boyfriend, but it bugged me that she was trying to keep me from even being friends with Koji.

I kept my mouth shut about him the rest of the week, and the ease between us returned as we made wire bracelets, painted mugs, and folded origami creatures. I decided I would try to find out what really happened on my own. Maybe then I could convince Charli that Koji wasn't a bad guy. At least I hoped he wasn't a bad guy.

But I didn't have investigative skills. Aside from doing a web search, which Charli had already tried, I hadn't found out anything that would help me convince Charli to chill.

By Friday, I was a little tired of art projects and missing the kitchen. How would I ever become a great chef if I never got to practice? Charli was probably getting closer to figuring out what kind of art she wanted to study while I wasn't any closer to figuring out how to wow my dad. Apparently my soufflé pancakes hadn't done the trick.

I begged off meeting up with Charli on Friday so I could go to the library and browse the cookbooks for a truly inspiring new recipe. I'd of course invited her to come along, but she had a felting project she wanted to try.

As I rode my bike into the parking lot, a guy was locking up a bike to the rack. He straightened as I pulled up and my heart skipped a beat.

"Sana!" Koji said, showing that dimple.

Today, he wore a turquoise-blue tank top, gray cargo pants cuffed at the ankles, and white Chucks with no socks. He must be off from his job since he wasn't in uniform.

I hopped off my bike and slid it into the rack. Koji's smile made my knees feel wobbly like jelly.

"Hey," I said, my voice coming out more like a whisper that I barely recognized.

"Sorry I didn't text you," Koji said. "Work was busy, and then yesterday I had to help my mom out with errands while my sister was at work."

"Oh. It's okay." That was a lot to take in. He was responsible. He helped his mom. He had a sister. Nothing there that hinted that he was a bad influence. Also, he'd apologized for not texting sooner. That was kind of nice. He hadn't said when he was going to text so, really, he had nothing to apologize for.

"You heading in?" Koji nodded at my backpack.

"Yeah. You?" Wow. Way to go, Sana, two whole words. I was capable of full sentences. What was wrong with me?

"Yep."

Koji fell into step next to me as I walked to the front door, trying to think of something to say so I didn't blurt out the question on my mind: Had he been expelled and sent off to a juvenile detention center? I mentally shook my fist at Charli for putting stories in my head.

"Why are you here?" I asked. And then realized it sounded rude. "I mean, what books are you looking for? I'm going to cook for a lookbook. I mean, cookbook. I'm looking for a cookbook."

Great. So now I was babbling. I peeked at Koji, who grinned at me. Not in a mean way, but like he was amused.

"Just checking to see what new plant books the library has. I come every week."

Interesting. Someone who regularly used the library couldn't be all bad.

This library was tiny compared with the one I used to go to in San Francisco. Koji held the door open, and we stepped into the air-conditioned coolness of the one-story building. I quickly made my way to the cookbook section, and Koji followed.

"You don't have to come with me, if you don't want," I said. Argh. Rude. Again! I took a deep breath. "I mean, I don't want to keep you from looking for your books."

He shrugged. "I don't mind. Unless you'd rather be alone?"

"No, it's fine."

We smiled at each other. There. That was better.

I wandered the aisle, hoping something would catch my eye.

"So, you like to cook?" Koji asked in a quiet voice.

I nodded, running my fingers along spines. When I got to the Asian section, I stopped and pulled a few books out. But like

Dad's books, they seemed complicated. After a few minutes, I finally found a soup book that included a ramen recipe I thought looked doable.

Koji nodded to my shirt. "Ramen fan?"

"Magic Ramen is, like, the best ramen place in San Francisco." I followed Koji to the bookcase at the front where the library displayed new books.

Koji scanned the gardening section and shook his head. "Nope. Nothing new this week."

As we made our way to the checkout counter, Koji asked, "So, San Francisco, huh? Do you go to the city a lot?"

He leaned against the counter as I rummaged in my backpack for my wallet and library card.

"No. I mean, not lately. I used to live there."

"And you moved here? Must be tough. I lived in LA during sixth grade."

I was so surprised he offered up that information that I fumbled my wallet, and my library card dropped to the carpet. When Koji leaned over to pick it up, I dove forward, nearly knocking heads with him, and snatched it up before he could see the last name on my card.

"Got it, thanks." I smiled at him. "What grade are you?"

"Starting eighth grade. I go to Carmel Academy," he said.

We were in the same grade, but he went to a private school. That explained why I hadn't seen him at our school. I cleared my throat. "So, you lived in LA? What was that like?" I quickly scanned my card, standing in front of the monitor so he couldn't see it, then scanned the book.

"It was awesome. Tons of restaurants, shops, museums, shows."

"Why'd you come back, then?"

"My family is here."

I shoved my book and wallet into my backpack and we walked outside to our bikes. "You went to LA alone?"

"Kinda. I stayed with my uncle. My mom wanted me to have a strong male role model."

So many questions bubbled up in me. "What about your dad?"

Koji scowled. But a second later the dark look was gone, replaced by his smile, although without his dimple. "My dad left when I was in the fourth grade. It wasn't like he was around much before that anyway. It's just me, my older sister, and my mom."

"Oh." I didn't know what to say. "So did you like staying with your uncle?"

Koji's cheek dimpled as his smile grew wider.

"What?" I asked.

"You didn't say you were sorry."

"Oh. God, that's rude of me."

"Nah. It bugs me when people say they're sorry when they hear my dad left. I don't miss him. I don't even know him. For most of my life he was busy traveling for work. His job was way more important to him than his own family. So don't feel bad for me. I have all the family I need at home."

Interesting. I mean, my dad wasn't home a lot either, but I never resented him for it. I was proud of him. And I didn't think that Dad loved work better than us.

I unlocked my bike and waited as Koji unlocked his. I couldn't think of a way to smoothly ask for more details about why he went to LA.

"So now you know more about me than I know about you. Your turn," Koji said, tugging his bike out of the rack and hopping on. "Follow me."

# 7

Both Mom and Charli would totally panic if they ever found out I willingly followed a boy I barely knew to some mystery destination. But Piper Bay was small enough, and if he headed somewhere unfamiliar, I'd just turn and go home.

I hadn't forgotten Charli's warning or her worries. It wasn't like I didn't respect her opinion, but she was biased. I mean, yeah, Koji getting expelled was not a good thing, but I needed to hear his side of the story to make a decision. I just had to wait for the right moment to ask. Then I'd tell Charli the truth so she and I could both hang out with Koji all summer.

Koji stopped in front of a little bungalow two blocks from the library. A stout woman wearing a smock over jeans and a loose, long-sleeved blouse plus a huge sun hat knelt in a flower bed, pulling weeds.

"Hey, Mom," Koji said as he hopped off his bike and gave her a peck on the cheek.

Koji's mom stood and brushed off her hands on her gardening apron. "Hello," she said, smiling at me warmly. "I'm Mrs. Yamada."

"Hi. I'm Sana." I purposely left off my last name. I liked that Koji didn't know who my dad was. I wanted him to like me for me. "I guess I know where Koji gets his green thumb."

She nodded. "He loves the outdoors. Always has. He's got a gift with plants."

My heart twinged. I was dying for my dad to say something similar about my cooking.

"Speaking of," Koji said, "I'm going to show Sana the garden."

"Have fun!" Mrs. Yamada went back to weeding her flower bed.

I rolled my bike up the short driveway. Koji opened the gate and we both parked in front of the garage. Then I followed him to a tiny backyard garden.

"My babies," he said proudly. "Japanese cucumbers, Momotaro tomatoes, green onions, and a bunch of herbs, including that rosemary bush back there. Also lemon and plum trees." He pointed to two small trees along the fence.

"Wow. That's awesome." I remembered Charli's comment about his job being court enforced or something. "So that's why you have the job with the landscaping company?"

Koji nodded once, curtly, and led me to the back of the small garden.

"You have to try the plums." Koji plucked two plump purple fruits and handed one to me.

I tried again. "You're lucky to have a summer job. Are you saving for something special?"

It looked like Koji was going to try to avoid answering again, but he said, "I'm not getting paid."

Then it *was* a court-ordered thing or probation, maybe. My heart sunk. But people deserve second chances, right? "Oh, sorry," I said.

Koji shrugged. "Don't be sorry. I'm doing it as a favor to my mom. Mr. Perez is a family friend. He helped her get a job. So when he got a ton of new customers this summer after he was profiled in our newspaper, Mom asked me if I'd lend him a hand.

He offered to pay, but he's always been really good to our family. And me. Plus Mom said it would be a great learning experience, getting to work with plants. And so far it's a good gig."

"That's nice," I said. I was relieved. I couldn't wait to tell Charli that, no, this wasn't some probation thing and that Koji was doing a kind favor for both his mom and Mr. Perez.

"Try the plum," Koji said, his cheek dimpling.

I bit in and nearly swooned. The fruit was sweet and tart at the same time. I practically inhaled it, letting the sun-warmed juice run down my chin. "It tastes like candy!"

"Right?" He grinned and pointed at my face. "You have some plum juice on your chin."

I swiped it with the back of my hand, but then my hand got sticky.

"Come inside," Koji said. "You can wash up."

I followed him through the back door, where we both removed our shoes. I couldn't help staring jealously at the small yet totally functional kitchen space. It was way better than the dated room we had at home.

Koji's kitchen looked like it was made for cooking in. The sink, stove, and refrigerator were laid out in a triangle configuration and no more than three or four steps apart, making it easy to move from one station to the next. There was generous counter space and pristine white cabinets all within reach. An ocean-blue glass-tile backsplash brightened the kitchen, and a bay window above the sink was lined with small pots of herbs.

"Wow." Koji's voice pulled me out of my trance. "You look like you hit the jackpot. I guess you really do like cooking," he said, pushing the hair out of his eyes.

I nodded, still gazing at the kitchen as I tried not to look too obsessed.

Mrs. Yamada walked in the back door, and I stepped out of the way so she could wash her hands.

"Would you like to stay for lunch, Sana?" she asked as she dried them with a towel. "Nothing fancy. Just fried rice."

"Can we help you?" Koji asked, flashing me a smile and a wink. A wink! This boy winked!

"That isn't very good manners," Mrs. Yamada said. "Asking a guest to prepare her own meal."

"Actually," I jumped in, "I love to cook. Or at least I want to learn how to be a better cook. I'd really love to play sous-chef and learn your fried rice recipe."

Mrs. Yamada's eyes widened in surprise and she smiled at Koji. "I like your new friend."

My cheeks warmed with pleasure.

"If you're sure this is something you'd like to do, then I'd be happy to have your help."

Once I'd washed my hands, Mrs. Yamada handed me a pretty black apron with purple flowers. Koji was already taking ingredients out of the refrigerator and piling them onto the counter, so I spun to the counter and got to work.

"You know how to use a knife," Mrs. Yamada said, sounding impressed as I diced green onions.

"This is a really great one." The balance and weight were perfect.

"I work at Kitchen Gala and get a generous discount."

I nodded, returning my focus to my chopping. That was the fancy kitchen store with expensive cookware and small appliances Dad always complained about. He said real chefs didn't shop in such places and stores, like those were for people with money who cared more about appearances than function. Dad had really strong opinions. Although I knew he'd spent a lot of money on the set of knives he'd bought in Japan.

After we finished chopping, Mrs. Yamada had me measure out all the ingredients before cooking, just like Dad taught me. And she showed me a trick I'd never seen my dad use. She put a container of rice Koji had taken out of the fridge into a glass bowl and then poured a little cooking oil onto it. Then she used her hands to mix the oil into the cold rice. So instead of a big hard block she would have to break up in the pan, the rice would be much easier to stir while cooking.

Koji hefted a cast-iron pan onto the stove and turned on the burner. After Mrs. Yamada added oil to the pan, she called out for ingredients. I handed them to her one at a time, but when she was ready for the rice, she passed me the wooden spatula and said, "Just stir so nothing burns."

She trusted me enough to cook! I turned to grin at Koji, who was perched on a stool on the other side of the counter. He smiled back at me, making my heart flip into my stomach.

Mrs. Yamada stepped around me to the fridge and grabbed a couple of eggs. Out of the corner of my eye, because I did not want to burn the rice, I saw her expertly crack the eggs into a bowl one-handed, something my dad could do, too. She added ingredients I recognized, and by the time she was beating the eggs with chopsticks, I knew she was making tamago.

Unfortunately I couldn't watch her as closely as I would have liked, because she asked me to plate the fried rice while she heated up her tamago pan. Koji stepped right next to me, his arm skimming mine as he held a bowl over the pan. My arm tingled as I scooped fried rice into three bowls.

As Koji and I set the kitchen table, I asked, "Is your sister going to eat with us?"

Koji shook his head. "Yuri is working today."

Mrs. Yamada set a plate of perfectly rolled tamago in the center of the table.

"Itadakimasu," Koji said.

I smiled and said the same phrase. We always said that before we ate at home, too.

And then, something else we had in common—we ate without talking. But it was a comfortable silence.

Dad complained that most people who dined at his restaurant talked too much, not taking the time or the care to appreciate the food. He said people should focus on using their mouths to taste and eat, not to talk, especially if they were spending good money on the meal in the first place.

Dad would totally appreciate the way the Yamadas ate.

When we were done, I turned to Mrs. Yamada. "Gochisousama. Thank you so much. This was a really delicious lunch. I love tamago and wish I could make it like you do."

"Oh, now you've done it," Koji said.

Mrs. Yamada smacked him playfully with her cloth napkin. "If you'd like," she said to me, "I'd be happy to teach you."

"Really?" I couldn't believe my luck. "I'd love that! That is, if you have time and it's not too much trouble."

"I'm off on Wednesday if you want to come back then," she said.

That worked perfectly. Both Mom and Dad would be at work. I'd just have to convince Charli that Koji was cool by then. Once I did that, I could tell Mom and Dad. Or least tell them about my new friend. Not about the cooking lessons because I was pretty sure Dad would not approve. "That would be awesome, thank you!"

I didn't want anyone, not Charli, not my parents, to keep me from coming back to learn how to cook from Koji's mom. Nothing was going to stop me. I'd learn the basics from Mrs.

Yamada, and then maybe I could learn how to make something high-end enough for Dad's taste.

This was how I would learn how to cook the perfect meal for Dad and finally convince him to cook with me again.

# 8

I couldn't help it. I knew Koji was at my dad's restaurant on Monday mornings, so I could see him there if I wanted to. Sure, Dad might come outside and catch me, which meant Koji would find out that my dad was the chef-owner of the restaurant, but it was unlikely. I'd overheard him telling Mom that on Monday the crew would be filming him making a few of his specialty dishes. That took focus and concentration. Dad would not be wandering around outside or checking on the landscaping.

If I were Dad I'd be dancing around and celebrating about being in a Baxton Ferguson (or any) documentary. But Dad had been reluctant to agree to be interviewed and featured. Despite being an über-popular chef with a packed restaurant, Dad was pretty humble. It was Mom who convinced him to say yes to Baxton. One night as I'd been reading in my room, I'd overheard Mom tell Dad in the kitchen that this was an opportunity for underrepresented people to see an Asian American chef who made a success of himself. That it was important for him to be a good role model. I didn't disagree. Dad said something about his parents, that had they been alive to see this, maybe then they'd think he wasn't a failure. That surprised me. I never met my dad's parents because they had died in an accident when Dad was living in Japan, before he met Mom. I wanted to know more about him and his past, but I could never ask. This wasn't the kind of discussions my parents had with me, and they would probably hate that I had eavesdropped. But now I knew enough to be sure that Dad would have a lot on his mind on Monday.

So that morning on my way to Charli's, I took the long roundabout path to her house that led right by Mikami Sushi. Koji was adorable and friendly. Totally worth the detour.

Charli would not approve. She would say that boys were a distraction, even though she'd had more than her share of crushes. She never did anything about them. What was the point of wanting something if you didn't chase it? She'd argue that she did when it came to her art. But I didn't see the difference. If you wanted something, you went after it. I was going to go after my goal of getting Dad to realize I was serious about cooking. And now that I'd met Koji, I wanted to get to know him better.

I was still arguing with Charli in my head when I made it to Dad's restaurant. The landscaping pickup truck was already there. As I walked my bike around to the parking lot, my heart sped up in anticipation, like I'd been waiting to see Koji forever. And when I spotted him, it went into overdrive. He was wearing the same backpack-tank contraption he'd used at the library to water the two boxwood shrubs that stood on either side of the back door.

When Koji saw me, he smiled with his dimple showing and stopped watering. "Hey! I was hoping you'd come by," he said.

That made me feel great. "What's with the tank thing?" I asked pointing.

"It's Mr. Perez's invention. We save gray water, like from our showers, to fill the tanks and use it in the gardens to conserve water."

"That's pretty awesome."

The white man I'd seen from the first day came around the corner. When he saw Koji and me talking, he shook his head. I didn't think Koji noticed, but he must have because he turned to the guy, his face empty of emotion.

"There are bags of mulch that need unloading," the man said and then spun back around and left.

Koji mumbled something under his breath that sounded like a curse word. I raised my eyebrows and he looked embarrassed.

"Ugh, sorry. That guy gets on my last nerve. He's always trying to be my boss and he's not. He works for Mr. Perez, and so do I."

"Ah." Although that man hadn't sounded mean or anything, I got it. Koji didn't like being told what to do, or what not to do, any more than I did. We had that in common.

Speaking of being bossed around, it made me nervous being so close to the kitchen. I was just getting to know Koji. The last thing I wanted was for him to think of me as the daughter of a famous beloved chef instead of a friend. I glanced at the back door uneasily.

"They're not open today," Koji said, noticing me looking at the restaurant. "You don't want to eat here anyway."

A burst of protectiveness for my dad overtook me. "Why not?"

He frowned. "It's overpriced sushi made by an arrogant chef."

My mouth dropped open. Okay, yes, the food was expensive, but not more than other high-end sushi restaurants. But arrogant? *Arrogant* was the last adjective I'd ever attribute to my dad.

Annoyance bubbled up inside me. I didn't like that he was saying untrue things about my dad. I was about to tell Koji the truth, even if it would embarrass him, but the look on his face froze the words in my throat. He looked angry. That didn't made sense. Why would he be angry at my dad?

There was a long awkward pause.

"I'd better go," I said as I climbed onto my bike. "My cousin is waiting for me."

"Okay. Oh, my mom said to come to the house at eleven on Wednesday. I get off work at noon so I'll be there for lunch." He smiled and it changed his whole face. The dark cloud had passed and was replaced by sunshine.

On my way to Charli's I made the decision to tell my cousin about him. I hated keeping this a secret from her. We never hid things from each other. She'd get that I needed to spend time with Koji and his mom to convince Dad to let me work in his restaurant, to teach me how to cook again. Mrs. Yamada's lessons could really help me.

I walked into the house and Charli was already set up at the kitchen table with her laptop and art materials. I slid into the seat across from her.

"So, I was thinking about Koji," I started.

"Sana!" she shrieked. "No!"

"Charli." I shot her a look. "Why can't we get to know him?"

She didn't let me continue. "Honestly, Sana. Do you have a thing for bad boys? Who are you?"

"I'm me! Your best friend and cousin. It's wrong to judge people without knowing the whole story. We need to find out Koji's side."

"There is no side! He punched my friend! He got expelled and sent away. Nothing he could say would change that."

"But why did Koji punch your friend?" I cocked my head at her.

Charli shrugged.

"You don't know? Or you won't tell me?"

"I told you, Koji was always arguing with everyone, even our teacher. He has a mean temper." Charli shook her head. "Just forget about him, Sana."

"Charlotte Boyce Hirai, you are not the boss of me!"

Charli took a breath. "Sorry. I know, I know! I just want you to be safe."

"I am! Koji has a job. He seems nice. You don't know his side of what happened and anyway, it was over two years ago." I couldn't tell her how he'd shared stuff about his past with me already. She was all wound up and would get all alarmed if I told her I went to the library with him and then to his house.

But without him, without Mrs. Yamada, I'd never be able to cook something impressive for my dad. I didn't want to tell Charli anything more until I could get her on board. If she was 100 percent against him, there was no way she'd be okay with me going to his house, even if it was to learn how to cook with his mom. And because she and her dad talked about everything, once Uncle Luke got wind of my plan, my parents would know. Dad would totally stop me from learning from anyone. I was sure he didn't teach me anymore because he didn't want me to cook at all. Maybe he thought I was too incompetent or unfocused. That was what he had shouted at me when I'd messed up the curry recipe, that I wasn't paying attention. That had been the last time we'd cooked together. No, to prove to Dad I could cook, I needed Mrs. Yamada.

Time to change the subject. "What are we making today?" I asked, nodding at the spread of colorful paper on the table.

"Paper flowers!" Charli brightened as she always did when it came to art.

We watched the how-to video in silence and then got to work. I was glad to have this distraction from our Koji conversation at least.

A couple of hours later we had two gorgeous bouquets of paper flowers.

"You can't even tell which bunch is mine and which is yours," Charli said. "You're getting better and better."

"Charli?" Uncle Luke called from the other room. "Can you come here for a sec?"

"Be right back. Make us something yummy to eat?" Charli said.

I hopped up from the table and rummaged around in their fridge. Unfortunately Uncle Luke was mostly a take-out and prepackaged meal person and they didn't have much in the way of ingredients. I found some processed cheese, a can of tuna, and fresh bread. At least they had my favorite Kewpie mayo. I could make tuna melts. I hoped to find some onions or tomatoes but nope. Just a clove of garlic sprouting in a basket. Koji would probably plant it.

Just as I was about to open the can of tuna, Charli came running into the kitchen, yelling, "Stop! Don't cook! We're going out to lunch to celebrate!"

"Celebrate? What are we celebrating?"

Charli danced around the room, shaking her hips and punching the air, laughing with her head thrown back.

I grinned. Her enthusiasm was catching. "What? What?"

She stopped dancing and leaned onto the counter, her eyes shining. "I got into the Pasadena Art summer program!"

"But you said you didn't get in."

"I didn't! But someone had to drop out at the last minute and I was at the top of the wait list! I GOT IN!" Charli started dancing again.

Uncle Luke walked into the kitchen, smiling. "I see Charli's shared the good news. Let's drive into Carmel for lunch. We can swing by and pick up your mom on her lunch break."

"Wait," I said to Charli, my heart sinking. "What about our summer together? How long will you be away? And when do you leave?"

Charli bit her bottom lip, trying to hold in her joy. "Wednesday morning. Sorry."

"That's in two days!"

"I know!" Her happiness was too big to contain. "The program starts next Monday, but orientation is this Thursday and Friday. I need to get a ton of supplies and pack today and tomorrow, then Dad's going to drive me down. I already have a dorm room and roommate assigned. The program lasts for five weeks." Charli grabbed my arms. "Five weeks of learning techniques from the top instructors and guest artists! Five weeks of making art!"

I forced myself to smile. "I'm happy for you, Charli."

And I was. It was really great that she was going. But this meant that I would be without my best friend for most of the summer. I was really happy for her, but I was sad for me.

# 9

Saying goodbye to Charli on Wednesday morning was hard. I'd smiled for her, though, because I didn't want to bring her down. Now I was doubly happy I had my cooking lesson with Mrs. Yamada that morning.

When I arrived at Koji's house, she waved me into the backyard, telling me to park my bike inside the gate.

"Thank you again, Mrs. Yamada, for teaching me how to make tamago," I said as I followed her into the kitchen, making sure to take off my shoes at the back door.

"I love to cook," she said. "I was planning to make lunch anyway. You're being very helpful by being here."

I washed my hands and put on the apron Mrs. Yamada handed to me, the same one I'd worn on Friday.

"Grab a carton of eggs and green onions," she said. "I'm getting salt, sugar, mirin, and shoyu."

I itched to write everything down as she listed off items, but I knew it was better to learn by doing. Too bad I couldn't record the lesson on video so I could watch it later.

"I made some dashi earlier," she continued. "I'll show you how to do that another time."

Another time! My heart soared. I placed the ingredients on the counter.

"Mirin is rice wine for cooking, and—"

I cut her off. "Yes, and shoyu is soy sauce." My cheeks burned. "I'm sorry. It was rude to interrupt you."

She laughed softly. "No, it's fine. I like your enthusiasm. I'm glad you know the Japanese names for some of the ingredients."

Even though I'd read about how to make tamagoyaki, I didn't have a clue how to use the pan. Dad had cooked the rolled tamago recently, but I hadn't been able to watch since I was doing the dishes at the time. Usually he made the custardy atsuyaki tamago that topped his nigirizushi, which took a lot of time. I wanted to learn the homestyle kind that was rolled.

"I'll make it first and then you can try," Mrs. Yamada said.

She broke eggs into a bowl, added ingredients, and beat them with a pair of chopsticks, like Dad did. Then Mrs. Yamada placed the rectangular pan on the stove and used her chopsticks to oil the pan with a small square of paper towel. Another thing she did the same as Dad.

"This is the tricky part," she said, beckoning me closer. "You layer the egg to make it thick and fluffy."

She spooned a thin layer of egg into the pan, tilting it to make it even. As it cooked, she used her chopsticks to nudge the cooking egg, rolling it to one end of the pan. She oiled the pan again and poured in another layer of egg, rolled the cooked egg over the cooking liquid, going back and forth layer by layer. When she was done, she had a beautiful multilayer rolled tamago that looked just like the photos I'd seen online.

"Gorgeous," I exclaimed.

Mrs. Yamada smiled as she slid the tamago on a plate. "Your turn!"

I mixed the ingredients, but it was hard to beat eggs with chopsticks. It seemed to take forever. But when I was done and ready to cook the eggs, I was giddy. I was finally going to make tamago on my own!

Copying Mrs. Yamada, I spread the oil onto the pan, and then ladled in a small amount of egg. As it cooked, I used my chopsticks to try and roll the egg. Except it was harder than it looked. I groaned as my chopsticks tore the egg.

"Don't worry, Sana," she said gently. "The bottom layer doesn't matter so much. Also, you've never made tamago before so don't expect perfection. Like learning anything new, cooking takes practice."

I kept at it, and when I was done, I had a lumpy blob that didn't at all look like tamago. Mrs. Yamada took the pan and slid my glob of an omelet onto the plate next to her perfect one.

"That was an excellent first attempt, Sana." She put the plate into the fridge to chill.

I tried very hard not to seem upset because I didn't want Mrs. Yamada to think I was too immature to teach.

"Oh, Sana," she said with a light touch on my shoulder. "You look so angry. Don't be hard on yourself. It took me many tries and, in fact, months before I was able to make a perfect tamagoyaki. You can do it. I can tell by the way you cook that you have a natural talent."

I raised my eyebrows.

Mrs. Yamada laughed. She had the same dimple on her cheek that Koji had. "I'm not just saying that to be nice. Koji can't even use hashi to roll the tamago. He uses a rubber spatula."

"Hey, don't talk about me behind my back!" Koji walked into the kitchen, a smile on his face.

My heart leapt in my chest. Because he startled me and *definitely* not because he looked good in his snug T-shirt. He took off his cap and even though his hair was plastered to his head with sweat, he still looked cute.

"Okaerinasai," Mrs. Yamada said.

"Tadaima," Koji answered, slipping off his shoes before he stepped all the way into the kitchen.

I was familiar with the Japanese welcome-home greetings, but we never used them. When we lived in San Francisco, I stayed at Alana's every day after school until Mom picked me up after work. Dad got home past ten or later the nights he worked at the restaurant. It was rare that anyone was fully awake or home to use the phrases when someone else came home.

"Hi, Sana," he said as he passed me to wash his hands in the sink. "Is lunch ready?"

"Almost," Mrs. Yamada answered, not noticing his gaze was on me. "Go get cleaned up."

Koji saluted and disappeared around the corner. Mrs. Yamada

took our tamago out of the refrigerator and sliced them on a cutting board. Mine didn't look as horrible as I feared. I mean, it wasn't pretty, but after it was sliced, I could see layers at least.

"It will be delicious," she assured me. "That is always the most important thing."

Dad wouldn't agree. He always said presentation was just as important as taste, but I supposed I had to start somewhere.

Koji rejoined us wearing jeans and a mint-green T-shirt with a graphic of a potted plant. As he sat down next to me, I got a whiff of fresh-cut grass. Shampoo? Or maybe just how he naturally smelled? It was . . . nice.

Mrs. Yamada placed our sliced tamago on the table, along with bowls of rice, Japanese pickles, and miso soup.

"It was my first time making tamagoyaki," I said, trying not to sound defensive.

"Looks better than my tenth attempt," Koji said, using his chopsticks to pick up three pieces of my tamago.

I smiled as I took two of Mrs. Yamada's and one of mine to compare the taste.

"It's good, Sana!" Koji said.

He was right. Not that I was full of myself or anything,

but it tasted the same as Mrs. Yamada's. Maybe I had what it took. Even though I was learning homestyle cooking and not fine-dining menu items like Dad preferred, maybe, just maybe I would be able to impress him enough to take me under his wing again.

# 10

After we finished eating, Koji washed the lunch dishes while I dried. Mrs. Yamada disappeared before I could ask if she would teach me to make something else next week. She'd mentioned showing me how to make dashi. I hoped she meant it and wasn't just making polite conversation.

"Thanks," Koji said a few minutes later as he took the drying towel from me and hung it up on a hook.

"Um, you're welcome. I guess I should go." I couldn't hang out much longer without it being awkward.

"Do you want some lemonade?" Koji asked. "I made it myself using the lemons from our tree."

"Sure. Thanks!" I was glad to have an excuse to linger, not only to wait for Mrs. Yamada, but also because . . . Koji.

"Are you leaving, Sana?" Mrs. Yamada said, reappearing in the kitchen doorway.

"Not yet," Koji said. "We're going to have some lemonade in the backyard."

We were going to have lemonade! In the backyard! Together! I tried to tamp down the joy I felt, not wanting to be too obvious.

"Oh, that's nice," she said. "If you want, Sana, I'd love to continue to cook with you on Wednesdays, but no pressure."

"That would be awesome," I said. "Only if you have time and I'm not a bother."

Mrs. Yamada smiled. "I can tell you are being raised by good Japanese parents."

"Mom!" Koji said, shaking his head. "Don't say that! That's a stereotype."

She shook her head. "No. It's true. Japanese kids need to be raised with proper manners and respect."

"That's *all* kids, Mom," Koji said. "Not just Japanese kids."

She waved her hand at him.

"Anyway," she said, turning back to me. "Should I call your parents to make sure they're okay with our cooking lessons?"

Ack! "No," I nearly shouted. "I mean, they're good with me coming here." Okay, that was a total lie, but in my defense, I panicked. I had never outright lied to my parents or kept things from them, but there was no way I was going to risk giving up this opportunity. Plus Dad would frown on my learning home-style cooking. He was all about fine dining. But then if he'd kept teaching me how to cook his way, I wouldn't need to sneak off to learn from someone else! "I'll let them know I'll be here on Wednesdays."

"Are you sure?" Mrs. Yamada looked concerned. "Won't they want to meet me?"

Saying no might make her think I wasn't being raised by good Japanese parents after all, but that was one risk I was willing to take.

"My parents trust me," I said. It was the truth, though it wouldn't be for long if they ever found out about this.

I followed Koji out to the backyard, where he led me to two chairs in the shade facing his garden. He handed me a glass of lemonade and we sat next to each other. Even though it was a very warm day, it was pleasant in the shade. I took a sip from my glass, the ice tinkling.

"This is really good," I exclaimed. "Tart with just the right amount of sweet."

Koji tossed his head, flipping the hair out of his eyes. "Thanks! A great compliment from a great chef."

That made me feel like a star! I gazed at all the lush greenery, impressed. "Your garden is really pretty. We have a very sad yard. Brown grass and patches of dirt, pretty much."

"I can come by and give you some pointers if you'd like. Maybe even help you fix it up."

It would be so great to hang out with Koji and work on our yard together. But unfortunately not possible since my parents couldn't know about him.

"Hmmm," I said. Then I noticed something about his garden. "Do you have any flowers?"

"Only when the fruits or vegetables are flowering. I'm mainly interested in plants that turn into food." He flashed a smile at me. "I'm sure as a chef you can appreciate that."

I nodded.

"Do you like flowers?" he asked.

"Yes."

"Cool. Do you have a favorite?"

"Hibiscus. Especially the bright red ones. My dad once gave

me one as a special gift a couple of years ago. I put it in a vase on my desk. It really brightened up my room. Anyway, hibiscus flowers make me happy."

Koji was so quiet that I turned to see if I'd put him to sleep. But no. He was watching me with a smile. My cheeks flushed, probably the same color as a hibiscus.

"I'm off tomorrow and Friday," Koji said, suddenly. "Do you want to come over? We can use the kitchen."

I pondered. Now that Charli was away, spending time with Koji would make for a better summer for sure. Both Mom and Dad worked those days. I could get away pretty easily.

"We wouldn't be alone, if you're worried about that," Koji said, interrupting my thoughts. "Either Mom or my sister, Yuri, will be around."

I blushed, realizing I'd taken too long to respond. "Oh no. I mean, that's fine. I'd love to come over. My cousin went away for a five-week art program, so I was kind of bummed that I'd be alone."

"You can hang out with me." Koji smiled and his cheek dimpled.

Suddenly my summer was looking perfect.

The back gate creaked open and clanged shut. A girl with blonde hair stepped into the yard. When she saw me, her face clouded over.

"Hey there," she said, striding up to us.

Koji turned around. "Hey, Harley."

The girl came around and planted herself right in front of me. I got a good view of her long legs in short shorts. Her pastel-pink shirt was just short enough to show a sliver of her pale flat tummy.

Harley put a hand on her hip and cocked her head at Koji. "Who is this?" Her voice was frosty, lowering the temps at least ten degrees.

"This is Sana," Koji said. "I met her last week."

"Hi," I said.

She didn't answer me and instead made a pouty face. "I have nowhere to sit."

Was she ignoring me on purpose? Koji made a move to stand, but I beat him to it. "I have to go anyway," I said. I handed him my empty glass.

Harley finally smiled.

"I'll text you later," Koji said to me.

It was my turn to smile. I grabbed my bike and left for home with a million questions boiling in my head. Who was Harley and how did she know Koji? I didn't recognize her from school. Did she go to his private school? Was she the unfriendly type or was she just unfriendly to me? And most importantly, why did Harley feel comfortable enough to waltz into Koji's backyard like it was home?

# 11

When I woke up the next morning, I remembered that both Mom and Dad were working all day so I could use the kitchen.

My stomach rumbled. I considered making tamago to practice what Mrs. Yamada had taught me, but I was hungry *now*. Best option? Omusubi. Besides, rice balls were my favorite go-to quick meal.

I opened the fridge and poked around, pulling out containers of leftovers. After placing them on the counter next to the rice cooker, which was warming rice from last night, I moved to the pantry to grab a can of Spam and a package of nori.

And then I got to work cutting precise rectangles from the sheets of seaweed. I used to rip the nori into pieces to wrap around the rice balls, but Dad taught me that presentation was important.

As I was shaping the rice ball, I was reminded of Charli and her art projects, and how she could look at simple objects and turn them into a masterpiece. She saw the possibility in everything. We used to lie in the backyard looking up at the clouds, and she'd make a game of finding pictures in their shapes. My heart twinged. Who'd have thought I'd ever miss doing crafts with my cousin? I had wanted a break from doing them every day, but now that she was gone, I missed her, of course, but I also missed doing projects with her and pushing myself to be creative.

Because I was distracted, I ended up with a misshapen rice ball. I held it up and, like Charli and I used to do with the clouds, I saw something in the shape. Working quickly, I snipped the nori and placed pieces of it onto the rice ball. I grinned as I held up an omusubi that looked just like a penguin. Then I made two more.

"Kawaii!" They were adorable!

I squinted at the can of Spam and another idea came to me. Slicing the meat into circles, I cut smaller ovals from the nori, shaped the rice, and soon I had three piggies. I snapped photos of my creations. My stomach rumbled again, and I took a bite of one of the Spam musubi piggies.

Delicious!

My phone chimed with a text. I'd tell Charli how she inspired me to make art from rice balls.

But it wasn't Charli. It was Koji.

**Koji:**
Hey! You want to come over?

**Sana:**
Sure! I can bring you lunch. I made too much.

**Koji:**
Excellent!

I cleaned up and then packed up the rest of the kawaii omusubi into a bento box, giddy to be able to share my creations with Koji. And yes, to see him again. I changed out of my pj's and pulled on a pair of shorts and the first T-shirt I found in my dresser.

When I got to his house, Koji was hanging around the back gate.

"Were you waiting for me?" I asked.

"Kind of? I mean I was working in my garden, but yeah, I was also looking over the gate every two minutes."

We both laughed.

"I've been told I have zero chill," Koji said, grinning with that dimple of his. "Hey, I like your shirt!"

I glanced down. The tee had a picture of a kawaii sushi roll with the words THIS IS HOW I ROLL on it. Appropriate for the occasion!

"Thanks," I said as I grabbed the wrapped bento from my bike basket and followed him into the house. Mrs. Yamada was washing dishes.

"Hello, Sana!" she said, turning off the water to greet me. "Koji skipped lunch, saying you brought him something?"

"I should have said there was enough for you, too, Mrs. Yamada."

Koji and his mom sat down at the table as I unwrapped the bento.

"These are lovely," Mrs. Yamada exclaimed.

"Whoa," Koji said, reaching out for the penguin musubi. "They're like works of art!" He took a big bite. "And delicious."

"Koji, manners!" Mrs. Yamada swatted at him for talking with his mouth full. That made me smile. She turned to me. "These are very good, Sana. You're so clever."

I basked in the warmth of her praise.

And in those short few minutes, Koji polished off everything I'd brought. Whoa!

"Do you want to make something else?" Koji asked.

Mrs. Yamada stood. "My kitchen is yours, Sana. Help yourself to anything. I have to run errands. Yuri should be home soon."

I blushed, thinking that Mrs. Yamada thought we'd need a chaperone. But I quickly forgot about that when Koji brought out a bunch of ingredients. He pointed to the rice cooker on the counter.

"From last night," he said, rubbing his hands together. "What are we going to make?"

My mind spun with ideas as I took in the ingredients on the counter: carrots, green onions, pink kamaboko, nori, slices of ham, and more. All those months of crafting with Charli had paid off because I immediately envisioned something.

"Rabbits!" I said.

"Okay," Koji said. "Just tell me what to do."

I scooped rice into a bowl to cool off and told him to cut the green onions long and thin. "Those will be the whiskers," I explained.

I cut triangles from the pink part of the kamaboko for noses. "Do you have nori? For the eyes?"

While Koji rummaged around in the pantry for the dried seaweed, I started to shape the rice into bunnies. I couldn't wait to show Charli my ideas.

"Hey, Koji?" I asked. "Can you take a video of what I'm doing? I want to send it to my cousin."

He held up his phone, hit record, and then started narrating like I was on some cooking show. "Now you'll note that Chef Sana has wet her hands and added some salt before shaping the rice. This keeps the grains from sticking to her hands, while also adding some flavor," he said.

I grinned at him and refocused on the task at hand. "You're absolutely correct, Koji," I said, getting into the act. "Now, I'm making round shapes for the rabbit heads, and I'll be using kamaboko, or fish cake, for the ears."

Koji leaned over and zoomed in on my hands as the bunny faces took shape.

Someone else might say we were being immature, but this was a lot of fun and I appreciated how comfortable Koji was goofing off around me.

"Check out the excellent detail of the kamaboko pink noses," he continued. "And how Chef Sana adds pink to the inside of the rabbit ears. Adorable, right, audience?"

Hearing Koji call me Chef Sana made me blush.

"What's going on in here?"

We both jumped as a teenage girl walked into the kitchen. Her shoulder-length black hair was damp, and she wore a white tank top with the words PIPER BAY POOL LIFEGUARD on it.

"Who are you?" she said when she saw me.

"Don't be rude," Koji said, ending the recording. He hopped off the counter and stood next to me. "This is my friend, Sana. Sana, this is my sister, Yuri."

"I wasn't being rude!" She peeked at the counter. "What are you making?"

"Rabbit-shaped omusubi," I said, using the tweezers Koji got me to place the whiskers.

"So cute!" Yuri said. "And I haven't had lunch yet."

"Again," Koji said, "shitsurei!"

"That's not rude," Yuri said.

I stepped back from my creations. "Help yourself. It's your food, after all."

"Ha!" Yuri snagged the plate and took it to the table.

Koji followed her, complaining. "Wait! I want to snap a pic!"

I stayed in the kitchen and started cleaning up.

"Hey, Sana," Koji called after he'd taken a picture with his phone. "Come join us at least."

I was still full from eating the omusubi I'd made at home. "Ugh, I can't eat another bite." I waved at the messy counter. "I don't mind cleaning up."

Koji gave his sister a look and she shrugged, popping a kamaboko ear into her mouth. "Mmm. Not only cute, but yummy!" she said.

Smiling, I dumped plates and bowls into the sink. Nothing felt better than having someone tell you the food you made tasted good.

"You're not a dishwasher, Sana," Koji said, joining me at the sink, bumping his hip against mine and nudging me out of the way. "You're our guest."

"I made the mess!" I bumped him back and reclaimed my spot in front of the sink.

"You two keep on flirting," Yuri called out. "I'm eating all of these."

Koji threw a dish towel at Yuri but missed by a mile. I laughed and started washing the cutting board.

"Fine, I'll dry," Koji said.

"With what?" Yuri called out. "The towel is practically in the next state!"

Koji grumbled good-naturedly as he fished a clean towel out of a drawer. "My mom is so happy she gets to teach cooking to someone who is excited about it."

"I'm happy to learn from her," I said.

Koji dried the last dish just as Yuri walked over and dumped her plate into the empty sink.

"Come over and cook anytime." She waltzed out of the kitchen, leaving me and Koji in a long silence.

Koji cleared his throat. "Are you free tomorrow? I'm off all day."

"Sure!"

"Don't eat lunch. We can make something here. If you want. It was fun today."

"It was!" I tried to keep my grin from spreading across my face like melting butter, already counting down the hours till I'd see Koji again.

# 12

"What are you doing home?" I asked Mom late the next morning. When I finally came downstairs, she was sitting at the kitchen table, perusing catalogs while sipping coffee, still in her running clothes. It was already ten a.m., which was the time her shift started at the hotel.

"Good morning to you, too," she said, smiling. She raised her eyebrows. "You look cute today. Where are you off to?"

I tried not to fidget under her scrutiny. Instead of my usual denim cutoffs and T-shirt combo, I'd chosen a mustard striped romper I'd bought with Charli at the start of summer. Mom wasn't supposed to be home. How was I going to get out of the house to see Koji?

"Just to the library," I said, the lie sliding out of my mouth way too easily.

Mom nodded. "Do you want a ride?"

Ugh. "Are you off from work today?"

"No. Just going in a little late. Cindy is on vacation, and they need someone to cover the evening shift. I told you this last night."

"Oh." I'd daydreamed through most of dinner, thinking about other kawaii rice balls I could make. And about Koji. "What are those catalogs for?"

"I'm going to start working on the house."

"What do you mean?"

"Fix it up. It's part of the rental agreement. Do you want to help?"

"But you don't know how to do that stuff."

Mom smiled. "Ah, daughter, ye of little faith. How do you think people learn how to do things? By doing!"

I agreed with her on that for sure. "Where are you going to start?"

"The half bath. It would be nice to have the door shut all the way."

We were using a big rock from the yard to keep the door closed when anyone was using it.

"*You* are going to fix the door?" I asked.

Mom laughed at my incredulous tone. "Well, Uncle Luke is going to help, but yes, I'm going to learn how to properly hang a door. I'm also going to replace the ugly linoleum with something nicer. Tiles, probably."

I blinked at Mom, like she might reveal herself to be an alien. "So you'll help?"

"What? No!" I laughed.

"Come on. It could be fun. A little mother-daughter bonding time."

My brain worked at superspeed. "Okay," I said. "I'll help you out on Mondays and Tuesdays when you're off. And I'll go to the library the other days. I think I want to study Japanese." Another half-truth slid out way too easily. I mean, I would have loved to learn Japanese, but that probably wasn't going to happen this year.

"Oh, that's wonderful! It's a deal." But then Mom frowned. "Won't you be lonesome this summer without Charli? Do you want me to see if there are any fun camps around Piper Bay?"

I shook my head so hard, my neck cracked. "No! I mean, it's nice, being able to be leisurely and all."

"I don't know. That's a lot of alone time."

"I'll be fine, Mom. I promise." That much was true at least.

"Okay," Mom said. "I trust you."

A sliver of guilt lodged itself in my heart. I'd be extra enthusiastic about helping Mom with her projects. That would make up for my tiny lies. Besides, I wasn't doing anything wrong, and the end goal was more time with Dad.

As soon as Mom left around noon, I texted Koji, who responded immediately with "Hurry over!" I laughed. He answered quicker than even Alana, the queen of texting, did. Like maybe he'd been waiting for my message.

Fortunately the library was on the way to Koji's house. I swung by it so that I could say I hadn't told Mom a full-on lie, and checked out a guide to beginner Japanese. Ten minutes later, I pulled my bike into Koji's backyard. I'd just raised my fist to knock when he swung open the door and grabbed my hand. His fingers were warm around my fist, making my legs go all melty like butter.

"Hey, no beating up the host," he said, laughing.

Even after he let go, I felt the imprint like a heat signature on my skin. But I shook it off as I followed him into the kitchen and got an eyeful of the setup. Koji had bowls of different ingredients spread out on the countertop, along with the rice cooker, two big plates, a cutting board, and knives.

"Whoa," I said. "So professional."

He shrugged. "I wanted you to have options." Koji tucked his chin, looking a little embarrassed and a lot adorable. "Also, I want to show you something."

He handed his phone to me and hit play. "Don't worry, it's set to private."

It was a video on YouTube. I held the phone up to see better and my eyes grew wide as the title played across the screen: "Cooking Cute with Chef Sana."

"We can work on a better title," Koji said, peering over my shoulder.

No words came to me as I watched the video unfold. It was the one he'd recorded of me the day before, making the kawaii rabbit rice balls, and it almost looked as good as the crafting videos Charli watched.

When it was over, I handed the phone back to him, still speechless.

He mistook my silence for something else. "I'm sorry," he

said. "I was just fooling around. It's not like anyone besides you or me will see it. I thought it would be a fun way to share with your cousin. You know, because you said to record your demonstration so you could show her . . ."

I finally found my voice. "Don't apologize. This is awesome!"

He smiled at me, making my heart skip. "Really?"

"Really." My mind spun. First, there was no way I could share the video with Charli without telling her about Koji and my cooking lessons. I'd need to talk to her about what I'd been doing first. But then I thought of something else. "What if we . . . kept going?"

"What do you mean?"

"My cousin watches all these how-to crafting videos. What if we made one for kawaii sushi?"

Koji's eyes lit up. "That sounds awesome!"

"But we'll need to make some adjustments." I'd have to make sure not to show my face. Not that Mom or Dad watched a lot of YouTube, but I did not want to risk getting caught.

"Sure! You're the star!"

I laughed with pleasure. "Okay, let's figure out what the

videos should be like. That is, if you don't mind." It occurred to me that I was running with an idea much like Charli often did with her art projects. I didn't want to pressure Koji into playing cameraman and director if he wasn't into it.

Koji grabbed my shoulders and squeezed. It was almost a hug. "This is gonna be an awesome summer project!"

I started to put on my apron, but Koji stopped me. "Mom left us some lunch so we can eat first. Your creations can be a snack."

Just then, Yuri walked into the kitchen wearing her lifeguard uniform. "Koji is a bottomless pit. He eats constantly."

"Hey, landscaping is hard work."

"So is being a lifeguard."

"You pretty much sit in your chair the entire day," Koji said, smirking.

She shrugged. "But I have to be vigilant. That's pretty exhausting."

Koji took my arm and guided me to the table. "Here," he said. "Sit. You're the guest."

The table was set with bamboo placemats and chopsticks on ceramic cherry blossom holders. Each place setting featured a small white plate with blue bamboo designs and a tiny rectangle dish set above it. A pretty blue shoyu container sat in the middle of the table. It was as nice as any restaurant.

Yuri sat down just as Koji set a gorgeous tray of sushi in front of us. My stomach rumbled its approval.

Koji sat next to me and grinned. Knowing he and Yuri wouldn't take any before I did, I quickly used my chopsticks to pick up a few pieces of nigiri. As soon as we all had full plates, I picked up a piece of salmon nigiri and popped the entire thing in my mouth, without dipping it into shoyu. I wanted to taste the fish and the rice. People often thought that sushi was all about the fish, but the rice was just as important. I closed my eyes as I chewed. And then my eyes popped open.

"Did you get these at Mikami Sushi?" It was that good. But Dad wasn't open for lunch and this did not taste like day-old sushi from the night before.

Yuri dropped her chopsticks with a clatter and quickly picked them up. She shot me a glare that shocked me.

"We don't say that name in this house."

"Why not?" I asked, recalling that Koji had said something similar earlier. I was annoyed with my dad, sure, but I loved him and it upset me to think of anyone not liking his restaurant.

"Our mom used to work at Sushi Ko," Yuri said.

She and Koji looked at me like that should explain everything.

"Okay?" I said, still confused.

"How long have you lived in Piper Bay?" Yuri asked.

"I moved here at the start of last summer."

"Oh, that explains it," she said. "Sushi Ko was the sushi restaurant in town before the new place opened. But it went bankrupt and had to shut down, and our mom lost her job. All because of that other restaurant opening."

Dad had said there weren't any other sushi restaurants in the area, which was one of the main reasons he'd chosen to open his place in Piper Bay. Had he lied? I frowned.

"Right?" Koji said. "Totally sucks. Some rich dude sweeps into town with his super fancy expensive restaurant and shuts down the competition. Bad move."

Had Dad caused people to lose their jobs? Had he made someone lose their business? Dad always said competition was healthy, but I didn't think it was right to put people out of work.

"Anyway," Yuri said, snagging another piece of sushi. "That's why we don't mention that restaurant around here."

"I'm so sorry," I said.

"Don't be," Koji said. "It's not like it was your fault."

Maybe not directly. But now I knew I could never ever reveal who I really was.

Not if I wanted Koji to like me.

# 13

I contemplated the remaining nigiri on my plate. I'd lost my appetite, but I also couldn't waste it. Which led me back to my question. "So where did you get the sushi?"

"Our mom made them," Koji said proudly.

"She did?" I picked up another nigiri and ate it. "Wow. These are really good!" My appetite roared back as I chewed and savored. I'd bet even Dad wouldn't be able to find fault with Mrs. Yamada's work. "She was the chef at the restaurant?"

Yuri made a sound.

"No," Koji said. "The owner wouldn't even let her in the kitchen. She was the hostess. She really loved her job because she's a people person, but she would have been so much happier working with the food."

"Wow." That reminded me of Dad's ex-boss who also hadn't thought women could be sushi chefs. Maybe that's why Dad didn't want to teach me Japanese cooking. Maybe he felt the same way.

"Our mom wants to go to culinary school," Koji said.

"She could easily go now if she weren't so proud," Yuri said.

"Don't." Koji shot her a look, like he wanted to silence her.

Yuri ignored him and turned to me. "Our dad has beaucoup bucks. He pays child support and alimony, but Mom won't use any of it for herself. Anything left over after stuff for us, mortgage, or whatever, goes into our college funds."

"Yuri," Koji said, cutting her off. "This isn't stuff you share with people outside the family."

"Like you didn't talk about it with your Harley?"

At the mention of Harley's name, my stomach dipped.

"She's not *my* Harley. Stop that."

The tension coiled around the room like a snake about to strike. I focused on my lunch, amazed by how fresh and flavorful each bite was. The rice vinegar seasoning was subtle and there was some other ingredient I couldn't quite identify. Sesame? No. Something else.

"You look like you're studying for a test," Koji said, his voice light again.

"Just appreciating the flavors," I said, glad he and Yuri weren't fighting anymore. "Your mom's nigiri is excellent. And I've had a lot of sushi."

We finished eating in silence, although it didn't feel as comfortable and natural as the day before.

"So," Koji said once we'd devoured lunch. "You ready to make some kawaii snacks?"

Yuri huffed. Then she gathered her dirty dishes, dumped them in the sink, and grabbed a set of keys. "I'm going to the movies with my friends."

As soon as Yuri stepped out the door, Koji turned on some tunes—it looked like he was into alternative rock—and we cleaned up. I was glad for the loud music because I was still reeling from the shock of how Dad's business had caused Mrs. Yamada to lose her job.

When we were done, Koji turned down the volume and waved his hands at the counter. "Before you start, I guess we should talk logistics."

I nodded. But my head was still spinning with questions that had nothing to do with making videos. I was curious about Koji's dad. And Harley. Whoever she was to Koji, he talked to her about personal stuff, and I didn't like the bit of jealousy that buzzed in me when I thought about that. All of Yuri's comments filled me with questions, but Koji's reaction kept me from prying. I'd have to find another time and a gentle way of bringing the topic back up. Plus at some point I wanted to ask about his being expelled. Now didn't seem like the right moment, so I changed the subject.

"How about *This Is How I Roll* for the name of the show?"

"Like your T-shirt? Excellent!" Koji said. He grabbed a notepad from a drawer and wrote it down, then looked up at me. "What else?"

"Could we not use my name? And maybe just show my hands? What really matters is making the kawaii omusubi." I shrugged. "I mean, I've watched a lot of how-to videos with my cousin and usually they just show whatever it is the person is working on."

Koji nodded. "Okay. Makes sense. But are you sure? You're very photogenic."

I blushed. That was almost like saying he liked the way I looked. "I'm sure."

"You got it!"

"I'll narrate as I make the rice balls, but you can do the voice-over," I said. I liked the sound of his voice, and the idea of us being linked together, proof that we'd done this project together.

"Cool!" He puffed up, strutting around like a peacock, and we both laughed. "Okay, so what are you going to make today?"

"Little lambs," I said. I'd come up with several ideas the night before.

"Nice!" Koji picked up his phone to record and said, "I can edit in an opening and voice-over, so go ahead and describe what you're doing. Don't worry about making mistakes or anything. We can keep this casual."

I took some time to prep, and when I had everything the way I wanted, I scooped rice from the rice cooker and started narrating. "Make sure your hands are damp and sprinkled with a little salt," I said as I formed an oval for the body. "I'm using black olives to make my lamb." I sliced an olive, using half for the face and slivers for the ears, tail, and legs. Then I added thinly sliced green onion for the eyes.

"You'll notice the precision she is using. She's talented with the knife. Don't make her mad."

I laughed and Koji grinned back. Happiness bubbled up

inside me. I was cooking. I was with Koji. And we were having fun. Together.

"What a cute flock of lambs, Chef!" Koji exclaimed after I'd made five. "And I have no doubt they're just as delicious." He made smacking sounds and pretended to lunge at me.

I placed my hands over my creations. "Ah ah," I said, giggling. "Patience, my hungry friend. Next we're going to make a panda. Let's use nori for the ears and eye patches." I pointed at the sheets of dried seaweed.

Just as I picked up a can of bamboo shoots, which would make an excellent tree trunk, the back door creaked open. I expected to hear Mrs. Yamada, but a younger, less familiar voice called out.

"What's going on in here?"

Harley. She wore a cotton floral dress that made me glad I'd worn my romper, and frowned at me before turning a bright smile on Koji.

"Hey, Koji," she said in a weird singsong voice. She sidled up next to him, leaning against his arm.

He draped his arm around her shoulder. "Hey, Harley. What's up?"

I dropped my eyes and opened the can, hating that Koji's arm was around Harley. I tried to tell myself that it only meant they were friends, but it still bugged me.

"Oooh," she cooed. "Are you recording something?"

I yelped as I sliced my finger on the sharp edge of the can. Dashing to the sink, I ran water over my finger, angry at myself. In all the years I'd been in a kitchen, I had never ever cut myself. Following Dad's safety rules strictly was a priority—even back then I knew if I injured myself, our lessons would end. They'd ended anyway, but not because of carelessness. Only this time, I'd allowed myself to get distracted by Harley. That was my bad.

Koji hurried to my side, taking my hand and examining it. The bleeding stopped and the cut was shallow. Plus my hand in Koji's was the best medicine ever, both for the pain in my finger and the pain in my heart.

"Are you okay?" Koji asked.

"I'm fine," I said.

"Here." Harley stepped between us and handed me a Band-Aid.

"Thanks," I said, drying my hand and taking her offering. That was nice of her at least.

"Good thing I know where the first aid stuff is," she said.

Oh. It was her way of letting me know she knew her way around the house. Unlike me, who has only ever been in the kitchen.

I put on the Band-Aid, returned to the counter, and started cleaning up.

"Wait," Koji said. "We have to finish the pandas at least."

"Yeah. I want to see what you're doing." Harley peered at the ingredients. "What is all this?"

Nope. I wasn't going to keep going while Harley scrutinized my every move. "I have to go anyway. I didn't realize how long I've been here."

Koji came over to help me clean up, while Harley disappeared down the hall. She was definitely comfortable here.

"Come back tomorrow after lunch? I work till noon. We can finish the video. I want to see your pandas." He smiled at me and I couldn't help but smile back.

Then I sighed. Mom was off work on Saturdays. I'd been

sneaking around, but knew not to push my luck by disappearing while she was home. "I can't."

"Koji! Our favorite show is on! Come on!" Harley called from the other room.

"Tell your mom I'll see her on Wednesday." I slipped on my shoes and was out the door before I had to watch Koji leave the room to join Harley.

# 14

I went to bed earlier than usual after a quick meal of instant ramen. Normally on the rare occasion when I was on my own for dinner, I took full advantage and made a real meal, but the afternoon with Koji, and Harley, had left me feeling . . . tired.

When I woke up the next morning, the first thing I did was check my phone. Texts from Koji, my San Francisco friends, and from Charli! I felt a little guilty opening Koji's first.

**Koji:**
Good morning!
I edited the video. Here's the link. Set to private.
What do you think?
. . .
I guess you're not an early riser? LMK
when you see this! I hope you like it!

I smiled as I clicked the link that took me to YouTube. Wow!

The video looked really good, almost professional. Koji had made an opening title screen with "This Is How I Roll" set in bright, bold letters. And he'd edited the footage of our "cooking show" into a seamless how-to video. The sound of my voice narrating took a little getting used to, but Koji's voice-overs made me smile, and the heaviness I'd felt when I'd left Koji and Harley together lifted.

The first thing I wanted to do was send the link to Charli, but I couldn't without telling her I was hanging out with Koji. I opened the group text thread next.

**Alana:**
Sana! Come over this weekend!
Mom said you can sleep over.

**Esme:**
Party at Alana's!

**Liv:**
We will have so much fun!

That would be awesome! I'd ask Mom, but I was pretty sure she'd say yes. I hoped she had time to drive me to San Francisco.

Saving the best for last, I opened Charli's texts.

**Charli:**
I miss you! But also this place is epic!
My roomie, Kiran, is a second-year, and truly
awesome at pottery. She took me to throw
some pots (that's artist-speak for making
pottery on a wheel) and I had a blast!
. . .
You're sleeping in, aren't you?
Classes officially start on Monday
but we've been busy with full days of
orientation. I'm so beat I fall asleep by 9.
Call me when you wake up! I
have things to tell you!

I texted Koji back first.

**Sana:**
Spectacular video!

**Koji:**
I'm glad you like it!
I know you're busy today, but do you
want to record another tomorrow?

**Sana:**
☹ I can't. Family plans.

**Koji:**
Monday?

I smiled. Okay, so if he didn't like hanging out with me,
he wouldn't keep inviting me over. From what I could tell,

both times Harley had shown up it was uninvited. Or at least it seemed that way. I wanted to ask him about her, but that wasn't a conversation I wanted to have over text.

**Sana:**
Sorry. I have stuff I have to do w/ my mom.
I'll be there Wed for sure.
And maybe we can do another video on Th.

**Koji:**
Got it. See you Wed.
Can't wait to see what you and
Mom make for lunch. . . .
Hey, is it okay if I post the video?
See if we can get an audience?

My heart pitter-pattered in excitement. Or maybe nerves. I reminded myself that there was no way my parents or Charli would ever see it.

**Sana:**
Go for it!

**Koji:**
😃 👍

I couldn't squelch the happiness bubbling up in me. I called Charli and she filled me in on orientation, her dorm room, and her upcoming classes.

"You sound happy," I said, smiling.

"And I haven't even told you the best part."

"What?"

"Tomorrow I'm meeting with a raku master. That's a type of Japanese pottery that's used mostly in tea ceremonies."

"Oh?"

"When I threw pots with my roomie, Kiran, I felt so happy, like happier than I ever have been doing any of the other art projects I've tried. And I spent time using the school's library and learned about raku. I still have so much to learn about pottery, but my counselor, Jo, got me a meeting with a raku master tomorrow."

"Wow, Charli! That sounds awesome."

She giggled. "So, what have you been up to? You miss me, right?"

"Yes, I miss you." I really did. If not for Koji, I'd probably be super lonesome. I wanted to share my joy with her like she'd shared with me. We never kept secrets from each other. "Hey, so I ran into Koji—" and that was as far as I got before she shouted.

"What? No! I hope you ignored him. Stay away from him, Sana. Promise!"

I sighed. "Charli, maybe he's changed. Or maybe the fight was a misunderstanding."

"Doubtful! My friend said he didn't even say anything to Koji. Koji just walked up to him during lunch and punched him! For no reason."

Okay. So, no. I wasn't going to tell her we'd been hanging out. Yet. I really did need to find out the truth from Koji.

But I wasn't going to promise Charli that I wouldn't see him either. I was saved by a horrible and very loud buzzing.

"What is that?" Charli asked.

"I don't know!" I shouted over the sound. "I'd better go!"

"Okay, but call me later. You haven't filled me in on what I've been missing in Piper Bay yet."

I followed the deafening sound to the half bathroom, where a long black cord snaked out from the doorway. I found my mom wielding some kind of machine against the floor. I shouted until she shut the thing off. She straightened, and I noticed she was wearing goggles and a big smile.

"Good morning, Sana!" Mom stood up and brushed off her faded jeans.

"What if I'd still been sleeping?" I asked.

"It's close to noon. You should be awake by now."

I ignored that jab and peered around her. "What are you doing?"

"I pulled the linoleum up yesterday and I'm prepping the subfloor with this sander."

"Where's the toilet?"

"Outside for now. You'll have to use the other bathroom for the time being. Do you want to come with me to pick up the tiles I ordered this afternoon?"

I eyed the floor warily. "Does that mean I have to help you install them?" Mom seemed to be getting a lot of joy from this house reno stuff.

"Uncle Luke is coming over later since it's my first time laying tiles. There's a bit of prep involved." Mom removed her goggles. Her hair was dusty. When Mom went from business executive in San Francisco to part-time hospitality staff in Piper Bay, I thought it was a nice change of pace. I loved having her around more. But this was a bigger change than I expected. Mom as a home renovator? That was a switch for sure.

On the way to the tile place, I asked Mom, "What does Dad think of your new hobby?"

"He's just as skeptical as you are."

"Hey! I didn't say I was skeptical."

She peered at me over her sunglasses and then returned her attention to the road. "You didn't need to. I can see it all over your face. You'd make a lousy poker player," Mom laughed. "At least I don't have to worry about you lying to me. I'd see right through you."

I nibbled my bottom lip. Time to change the subject. "Is Dad done with the documentary?"

"Almost," Mom said. She pulled into the parking lot and slid into an open space. But instead of getting out of the car, she turned to me. "So tomorrow and Monday, the crew is coming to the house."

"What? Why?" I asked, breathlessly. "Can I hang out?" I would be super annoyed if my parents kicked me out of my own house.

"Of course." Mom laughed like it was a ridiculous question. I guessed she hadn't heard Dad basically forbid me from being in the restaurant while he was taping. "Baxton wants to film your dad at home with the family."

"I get to be in the documentary?" I squealed at the thought of being in a Baxton Ferguson film.

"No guarantees, but yes, he wants to interview both of us." Mom smiled.

"That's awesome!" Wait till I told my friends about this! Then I remembered my exchange with Alana and the others. "Oh, Alana invited me to stay over at her place this weekend."

"Oh, okay, so you're going to just pass on this?"

Before I could protest, Mom burst into laughter. I grumbled, "Don't tease!"

"Sorry," she said, not sounding sorry at all. "Why don't you invite them over here instead?"

"Baxton wouldn't mind?" My friends would be so excited to be around for filming.

"I'm sure it'll be fine. Mostly they'll be filming Dad, of course, so you and your friends can hang out in your room or watch if you stay out of the way."

"Perfect! Thanks!"

I was in such a good mood that walking through the tile store was fun. I fantasized about redoing our kitchen in a variety of blues that reminded me of the ocean, and Mrs. Yamada's kitchen. If Mom really got into this, maybe we could fix ours up. While I was daydreaming about island butcher blocks and farmhouse sinks, Mom picked out sand-colored tiles for the half bath that would brighten the small room for sure.

As soon as we got home, I texted my friends.

**Alana:**
That's even better than you coming here!

**Liv:**
We'll finally get to see your new home.

**Esme:**
WAH! I can't go tomorrow!

**Sana:**
No! Why not?

**Esme:**
I've got that dance recital. That's why having a sleepover would have been perfect.

**Sana:**
Sorry! Next time for sure!

**Liv:**
I just checked and my mom said she'll drive us. Her cousin lives in Monterey Bay so she'll visit while we hang!

**Esme:**
Yes, this is me pouting. But y'all have fun.

I would miss Esme for sure, but I was super excited my friends were visiting and that I wouldn't miss being here for filming. Not only would I finally get a peek into Dad's documentary, but maybe Baxton would ask me some questions and Dad would see how serious I was about cooking.

# 15

Let me be clear, I'm not typically a vain person. I mean, I like to look decent, but unlike my friend Esme, I'm not up on the latest fashion or in love with designer labels. And where Charli's artistic leanings mean she loves playing around with makeup, I'm basically a lip gloss kind of girl. So on Sunday morning, though I wished desperately that Charli was here to give me styling advice, I settled for pink lip gloss and an hour spent going through my closet. What outfit would say "future chef" best?

I finally decided on gray leggings and a light blue tunic top that kind of reminded me of a chef's coat.

"Sana! Your friends are here!" Mom called just as I heard the doorbell ding.

I dashed down the steep stairs, squealing as I spotted Liv and Alana, and wrapped them up in a big group hug. They kicked off their shoes—we'd all been friends long enough that they knew of our no-shoes-in-the-house rule—and followed me up to my loft. This was the first time they had been to Piper Bay.

"No fair!" Alana said. "Your room is huge!"

"And awesome!" Liv glanced out the window and waved to her mom as she drove away.

"I'd kill not to have to share with my little sister." Alana bounced on my bed, her eyes flitting around my space.

"Okay, spill!" Liv said, joining us on the bed. "Tell us everything. Texting is all surface stuff, yeah?"

"Well, you know how my dad isn't very supportive about teaching me Japanese cooking?"

Alana rolled her eyes. "He's still on that? Or NOT on that?"

"Totally unfair!" Liv agreed.

Oh how I'd missed my friends! "Well, I found someone else to teach me!"

"Really?!" Liv squealed. "Who? Where?"

"Not so loud!" I shushed her. In this small house voices totally carried. Fortunately Dad was at the restaurant doing all his prep early for tonight's service so he could come back to film at home later this morning. Mom was in the tiny backyard sweeping.

She'd already spent most of yesterday cleaning the house. For my part, I straightened my room.

I told Liv and Alana all about Mrs. Yamada.

"That's so awesome," Liv said. "But how did you meet her? And doesn't it feel kind of weird to be hanging out with someone your mom's age?"

I took a deep breath, and told my friends about Koji. Finally I could let my big secret out!

Liv and Alana squealed so loudly that my ears rang.

"Do you have a picture?" Alana asked.

I shook my head. "But you want to hear his voice?"

"Um, yeah," Liv said. "Only . . . how do you have a recording of his voice and not a photo?"

I grabbed my laptop and opened the YouTube video. "You have to promise not to tell anyone about this!"

"But Esme."

"Of course, yes, tell Esme, but swear her to secrecy!"

"Done!" Alana said, and she reached around me and hit play.

I watched my friends' reactions since I'd already watched the video over a dozen times. It thrilled me to be cooking and to see proof of it.

"Those rice balls are adorable," Liv said. "You are so talented."

"Hello!" Alana said, waving her arms. "Who cares about the food? The boy! His voice! Super suave."

"Suave?" I burst out laughing.

"Make fun all you want," Alana said, swatting me, "but he could be, like, a voice-over actor for commercials or audiobooks. He has a swoony voice."

"You already have a boyfriend," I said, wrinkling my nose.

"Oh ho!" Liv crowed. "Does our Sana sound jelly?"

"She does!" Alana bounced on my bed with glee.

"I do not!" I made the decision right then not to tell them about Harley and my feelings about her.

"Hey," Alana shouted. "Look at the viewer counter!"

We all leaned in. And when I saw what Alana was talking about, my mouth dropped open. "312?" I squeaked.

"Over three hundred views," Liv said, almost breathless. "Sana, you're going to go viral!"

I laughed. "I doubt it." But still! Three hundred was a lot for a first video. Koji had just posted it a day ago. Pride mixed with happiness swirled inside me.

Alana pulled out her phone, tapped on her screen, and scrolled. "Quiz time!"

Both Liv and I groaned. Alana and her online quizzes.

"Sana," she said, using her best teacher voice. "Number one, do you think about him all of the time, most of the time, some of the time, only when you're with him, or never."

I knew that I had to answer because Alana would not let up otherwise. Liv shrugged at me. "Some of the time."

Alana raised her eyebrows at me. "Okay, most of the time," I admitted.

She grinned triumphantly. "Do you look for excuses to text him or see him?"

I sighed. "Yes."

"When you see him, does your heart speed up or do you feel warm?"

I put my head in my hands. "Stop! I don't want to answer any more questions." Alana gave me a look. "Fine. I guess I like him."

She and Liv got up and did this silly dance they do when they are right about something. "Sana has a crush! Sana has a crush!"

"Hold on!" Liv said. "It's more than a crush. He's a potential boyfriend!"

Liv and Alana sat down next to me again, hugging me from both sides. "Ohhh, Sana," Liv said. "A boyfriend."

"Stop," I said, feeling my cheeks get hot. "Don't put the pressure on. I like him. He's cute and fun and nice, all right?"

"All right." Alana and Liz smiled proudly. Oh brother.

"He's just a boy. The most important thing is that his mom is teaching me Japanese cooking."

"Right."

"Promise you'll keep us posted!" Liv said.

"And send us new links to your cooking show." Alana nudged me. "When's the next one going up?"

"Hmm. Later this week," I said.

Liv pulled out her phone and tapped. "I just subscribed."

Alana followed suit. "Me too!"

"Sana!" Mom called up. "The film crew is here!"

We scrambled down the stairs where Griff was adjusting the lights while Shelby walked around the house with the camera. Baxton smiled when we walked into the living room.

"Sana, thank you for agreeing to let me interview you," he said.

Alana and Liv gripped my arms in excitement. They perched

on the bottom of my loft stairs to watch as Griff and Shelby set up in the living room. Baxton invited me to sit on the couch, then sunk down across from me in Dad's chair.

"Don't worry about the camera," he said. "It's just you and me having a chat."

"Sure!" I wasn't worried at all. This was exciting!

"Okay!" he said. "Sana, tell me a little about Piper Bay."

I talked about going to school with Charli and how nice it was to be able to bike around town on my own.

"That sounds fun," Baxon said. "So, what's it like having a famous sushi chef for a dad?"

"Um, I'm super proud of him," I said. "He worked really hard and he gets to follow his dream." I cleared my throat. That didn't sound very important. It would probably get cut. I needed to say more interesting things.

"What about you?" Baxton asked. "Do you have dreams?"

There we go! "Yes! I want to be just like my dad!"

Baxton's face lit up, making me feel great. "You want to be a sushi chef, too?"

Just then Dad walked into the room. I hoped he'd heard me.

Maybe he'd say something encouraging on camera. It would be a record of his promise to teach me!

"Baxton," Dad said, not seeming to notice we were in the middle of an interview. "Did you want to film in the kitchen?"

"Definitely!" Baxton stood. "Are you ready, then?"

"Yes."

And that was it. Baxton thanked me, then he and the crew followed Dad into the kitchen.

"You were awesome, Sana!" Alana gushed.

I didn't feel awesome. I wondered if any of that would make the cut. It was obvious Dad was so against me cooking that he didn't want me in the kitchen or even talking about cooking!

Mom would make the cut though. I watched as Shelby filmed Mom working on the tiny guest bathroom. She got really animated talking about renovating the house. Kind of how I would have sounded if I had been allowed to talk about my passion for cooking food.

By the time Dad and the crew were done, it was hard to put on a happy face for my friends, but I did. Even though inside I was full of scorching disappointment.

# 16

When my alarm went off on Monday morning, I groaned, but got up and headed to the shower. The crew was returning to film Monday Breakfast. I wasn't as motivated to look camera ready today since yesterday I'd hardly been in front of the lens at all.

I quickly dried my hair, threw on jeans and a Mikami Sushi T-shirt. Dad didn't love the idea of a restaurant T-shirt. He thought it made it look like he was trying to get attention for the "wrong reason." It was the same thing he'd said when he hadn't wanted to be in this documentary. He wanted to be known for his sushi. But Ruthie Moon, the hostess at Mikami Sushi, convinced Dad a T-shirt would be good for the business. Ruthie was no ordinary hostess. She also did the books, designed and updated the website, and handled reservations. She was brilliant with marketing, which was something

Dad was not into at all. And she had been right. A lot of customers bought a shirt after dining there. As Ruthie said, free advertising.

When I walked into the kitchen, Baxton and his crew were setting up their equipment.

"Good morning, Sana," Baxton said.

"Hi!" I leaned on the counter. At least I'd get a delicious breakfast out of this.

Dad walked in, tying on his apron.

"Chef Hiro," Baxton said, "I'd like to film you cooking breakfast with Sana."

Dad's eyebrows went up and his mouth fell open a little. I think I might have looked the same.

"I don't know," Dad said. "Maybe not such a good idea."

"Why?" Baxton asked.

"I don't want to put Sana on the spot," Dad said. He actually looked concerned, which confused me.

"I'm totally happy to help you, Dad," I said quickly.

When Dad hesitated, I knew I had a chance. I just had to convince him.

"I haven't forgotten anything you taught me," I said. "I will be the perfect sous-chef and do everything you ask, without question. I'll pay attention. I'll stay focused."

*I won't screw up like I did the last time you cooked with me.* I didn't say that out loud, of course.

"Great!" Baxton said, waving Griff and Shelby over. "It's decided!"

I grinned as Dad started setting out ingredients. I stayed out of the way, on the other side of the counter.

"I want to get you two cooking *together*." Baxton waved me to join Dad.

Dad gave me a quick nod. Permission! I nearly sprinted to his side, my grin so big my cheeks hurt.

"We're going to make your soufflé pancakes," he said.

"My *what*?"

"Those pancakes you brought to your dad the first week of filming were amazing," Griff said as he moved a reflector shield.

I blinked. Dad had never mentioned them, much less sharing with the film crew. I felt like I'd just won a grand prize. Dad had eaten my pancakes. Not only that, he'd liked them enough to replicate them. And now he was cooking with me. On film!

"Okay, nothing formal, Chef Hiro," Baxton said. "I just want you to be a dad cooking with his daughter. Casual, fun. Just act like it's a regular Monday morning at home."

Dad and I exchanged a glance, knowing that this was not at all like a regular Monday. But instead of a stern or disappointed look, Dad smiled. A genuine Dad smile like the kind he used to give me when we cooked together back in our San Francisco home. It was as if someone had flipped a switch.

He nodded to the ingredients on the counter and, without any prompting, I started measuring. Then he placed a bowl in front of me and handed me two eggs. I separated them, proud of how cleanly I managed to do it without breaking the yolks. But when we both reached for the bowl with the egg whites at the same time, I jerked my hand away as if I'd been burned. I wanted to show Dad I could read his movements quickly and know what he wanted without him saying so, and I'd already messed up.

I nearly melted with relief when he laughed, like it wasn't a big deal at all. Dad slid the bowl with the yolks to me and handed me a whisk. I added ingredients and beat the mixture while he set up the stand mixer.

"Okay, I'm going to need a little bit of chatter from you both," Baxton said with some amusement. "What are you doing now?"

Dad started narrating what I was doing. I had a brief flash of me and Koji doing the same for our cooking show. But then I refocused. I had to prove to Dad I was a reliable sous-chef. This could be my chance to win him over for good.

"Beating the egg whites is one of the most important steps to making fluffy soufflé pancakes," Dad said. His voice was low but clear. Soothing. "Air bubbles are key. Over- or underbeat, and the pancakes will fall flat."

As soon as the egg whites stood in stiff peaks, Dad shut off the mixer. "Why don't you finish the batter, Susannah?"

"Really?"

He nodded. As I folded the meringue into the batter, he asked, "Why are you being so gentle with the meringue?"

I glanced at him, surprised that he was going to allow me to speak on camera. When he nodded encouragement, I said, "I don't want to break any of the air bubbles."

"Exactly!" Dad said.

He heated the pan and stepped back. Wow. He was going to let me cook? On camera? I spooned batter into the pan, and we watched the pancake rise and bubble. Soon I'd made a big stack of them. Dad kept up the narration as he plated my pancakes, dusted them with powdered sugar, and garnished them with a mint leaf. We smiled at each other, Team Mikami.

Together, we walked the plate over to Mom, who was waiting at the kitchen table. Shelby zoomed in on Mom as she sliced into the pancakes. She took a forkful, and as she chewed, she closed her eyes. After she swallowed, Mom smiled and blew a kiss to me and Dad.

"And cut!" Baxton called. "That was fantastic! One-take perfection. Loved how your family dynamic just shined through. It's obvious Chef Hiro and Sana are accustomed to cooking together. Bravo!"

Griff and Shelby started to pack up. I couldn't wipe the grin off my face even though Baxton was totally wrong about how Dad and I spent time together in the kitchen. But maybe this was a sign. Maybe this was Dad's way of telling me that he had changed his mind. I wouldn't need to sneak around to take lessons from Mrs. Yamada!

That gave me pause. I didn't really want to give up learning from Mrs. Yamada (or seeing Koji). But maybe I could do both—learn high-end cooking from Dad and home cooking from Mrs. Yamada! Maybe Dad could make my dreams come true.

# 17

I'd told Dad I would do all the cleanup so that he could go back to the restaurant with the crew. They were wrapping up filming this week, and then Dad would go back to spending every free moment coming up with ideas for new dishes and working at the restaurant. But maybe now he would invite me to help out.

Not that he didn't have good help. His sous-chef, Ethan Jung, had followed him from the San Francisco restaurant. And Manny Mariscal was his line cook (and part-time college student studying microbiology). Dad still did a lot of the work, shopping, prepping, creating, serving, and cleaning, but he relied on Ethan and Manny to keep the restaurant humming. And I knew that while the documentary was being filmed, Ethan was stepping up. But there was always plenty to do in the kitchen. I would be happy just to be there.

As soon as Dad left with the film crew and Mom went to

meet the interior designer, I rummaged through the kitchen. I decided Dad and I could make dinner together, starting with things I already knew. Then he could ease into teaching me more complex dishes.

We had the ingredients for tonkatsu. The fried pork cutlets were one of Mom's favorites. Dad used to make it almost weekly back in San Francisco. I wasn't sure if he decided it was too low-brow for him now that he ran a fine-dining sushi restaurant or if he was just too busy these days.

I opened the pantry. Wait. Where was the oyster sauce? It was an ingredient for Dad's homemade tonkatsu sauce.

I glanced at the clock. If I biked to the restaurant, I could grab a bottle of oyster sauce, catch Dad before he got too focused on inventory, and ask him when he would be home that evening. Since he was closed on Monday he should be back at a decent hour.

But when I got to the restaurant neither Dad's car nor the film crew's truck was in the lot. I did recognize Ruthie's mint-green Vespa though. I knocked at the back door.

"Sana! It's great to see you!" Ruthie was bubbly and enthusiastic, the perfect foil to Dad's stoic demeanor. She was the big sister I would want if I had one. More than once a customer has asked if we were related. Just because we were both Asian. We looked nothing alike, and anyway I was Japanese and she was Korean.

I stepped into the kitchen. "Dad's not here?"

"He was but then he left. The crew is filming B-roll around town and going to the beach. But they'll be back."

"Oh, good!" I followed Ruthie into the restaurant where she had her laptop open on the bar. "What are you up to?"

"I accidentally left my phone here last night so I came to pick it up. Plus my roommates were being noisy, so I figured I could get some work done while I was here. I'm tweaking the website. Your dad is extending restaurant hours this summer to allow for additional reservations."

"How late?"

"Just a little bit. Last reservations would be at nine thirty instead of nine."

I frowned. That would mean he wouldn't be home till at least eleven.

Ruthie smiled and gently patted my shoulder. "I know you want to see your dad more often, but this is a good thing. He's doing great! And with the documentary, whenever it releases, he'll end up being even busier."

I sighed.

"He'll probably have to hire an additional chef," Ruthie said. "Ethan could use a break, but then again, he might be striking out on his own soon."

That was typical for sushi-chef apprentices. Ethan has been with Dad for over five years now. Dad had had to apprentice for ten years in Japan.

"What about Manny?" What I really wanted to say was, what about me? But I knew Dad would never go for that, and yeah, I knew I was too young. But if Manny got promoted, then Dad would need another line cook, and maybe I could do that. Or . . . something.

Ruthie smiled. "He doesn't want to work in a restaurant forever. But he loves working for your dad."

Well, it wasn't as if Dad would have really hired me anyway. Even if I wasn't his daughter, I wasn't old enough for a full-time job.

"I'll be in back while I wait for Dad. And I won't mess anything up."

Ruthie laughed. "I know."

I slipped into the tiny kitchen and spun in a slow circle. Someday, maybe, Dad and I would be working in here side by side. He'd let me invent my own sushi. Dad was traditional. He created his menu around what was in season, which fish was the freshest. No fancy rolls here. Almost everything was nigiri, and there were no side dishes or appetizers. Customers got nigiri, and tea, water, or sake. For dessert, fresh fruit, yokan, or in the summer, shaved ice.

He made one exception. The signature Hiro Roll. It was the only roll he made—and you could only get it during omakase meals.

I put on a clean apron and held an imaginary knife, pretending to slice fish for sushi. In my head I heard Koji narrating, "Here is the famous sushi chef Sana Mikami preparing her famous dish." I smiled at the imaginary camera.

"Susannah, what are you doing back here?"

I nearly leapt out of my skin. I'd been so lost in my fantasy that I hadn't heard Dad come in.

"Hey, Dad." I peered around him, hoping my cheeks weren't red with embarrassment. "Where are Baxton and the others?"

Dad waved his hand at the apron, and I hunched my shoulders as I removed it, hanging it back on the hook. "They're taking a break while I get dinner ready."

"Dinner?"

"They will be done filming this week and I wanted to make them a special meal."

"Here?"

"Of course, here."

Oh. So he wouldn't be home for dinner after all. My hopes of cooking tonkatsu together were dashed. But we could still cook together. We'd proved we made a good team this morning.

I brightened. "I can help you!"

Dad raised his eyebrows. "That's okay. I've got this. I have everything in my head."

I slumped. Right. I would just be in the way.

"Go home and have dinner with Mom."

Fine. I turned to the shelf with all the sauces and scanned it until I saw what I wanted, and grabbed the bottle of oyster sauce. "I need this," I said. "We're out at home."

"Are you cooking?"

I straightened my shoulders. "Yes."

Dad nodded and walked over to the hook to grab his apron. Without turning back to me he said, "Make sure you clean up."

He got to work, and I knew that that was the end of our conversation. He hadn't asked me what I was making, but he also hadn't told me I couldn't use the kitchen. It was almost as good as having his blessing. I took solace in that and biked home with a renewed determination to continue my lessons with Mrs. Yamada no matter what.

# 18

Mom loved my tonkatsu dinner on Monday and let me cook again on Tuesday, but Dad hadn't made it home till late. I'd left him a plate both nights and it looked like he'd eaten—the meals were gone in the morning—but he hadn't said a word to me about them. Maybe he thought Mom had made the dinners, although she never cooked Japanese food. She said she got nervous cooking for Dad even though he never criticized her. So she played it safe by making things like spaghetti and meatballs and roast chicken with potatoes. The only time the three of us cooked Japanese food together was for New Year's Day, so naturally it was my favorite holiday.

But I didn't want to wait months and months to get back into the kitchen with someone who actually wanted to teach me. On Wednesday, Mrs. Yamada was waiting for me.

"Today we're combining the two things we've already made,

egg and fried rice. This is Yuri's favorite meal—omurice."

"What's that?"

Mrs. Yamada raised her eyebrows at me. "You've never had omurice?"

I shook my head.

"It's usually a home-cooked meal, though sometimes it's served in diners."

Oh. That made sense. If this dish was diner food, it was very unlikely Dad'd ever make it. He didn't even like making hamburgers.

"It's basically fried rice with an omelet on top, dressed with ketchup." She smiled. "While it may not sound like much, it's quite delicious."

"I bet it's yummy!"

"First I'm going to teach you how to make dashi. It's the base for many Japanese recipes."

I knew that. Dad made his own dashi every morning for the restaurant, but other than knowing it had kombu, or dried kelp, and bonito fish flakes in it, I had no clue how to put the stock together.

It turned out to be pretty simple and I was thrilled that I now could make dashi on my own. And the omurice was easy, too. Mrs. Yamada showed me how to make fried rice Yuri's favorite way, with peas and salmon.

By the time Koji walked in, we were plating. Yuri came out of her room to join us. Mrs. Yamada drew pictures with the ketchup on top of the omelets. A flower for Koji, an ocean for Yuri, a sushi roll for me, and a smiley face for herself. So cute!

After Yuri left for work and Mrs. Yamada went to work in her garden, I told Koji my newest idea for our show. "I was watching some videos and I think I can make a sushi roll that looks like a flower." I shrugged at him. "I mean, I know you don't really like flowers—"

"I like flowers!" Koji said. "I only said I haven't really grown any. Yet."

"Okay, then."

"This sounds great! Let's talk about the details outside." Koji tucked the notebook under his arm and grabbed his lemonade. I picked up my glass and followed him into the backyard.

I sat down in the same chair as before, but this time Koji dragged his snack next to mine and balanced the notebook on our two armrests.

"Okay, what all will you need? We've got rice—Mom makes it every night—and all the rest of the usual stuff. Do you need anything special?"

"I'm assuming your mom has bamboo mats for rolling and rice vinegar. I'll need those skinny cheese sticks and beet juice, but I can bring those."

"It's okay! I've got it. You're doing all the work. I'll provide the ingredients."

"Are you sure?"

"I'm sure." Koji nudged my arm and smiled.

I checked my phone and realized I needed to get home before Mom. "I'd better go," I said, standing.

Koji walked me to my bike and then opened the gate for me. "See you tomorrow!"

"What's tomorrow?" Harley stood on the other side of the gate wearing a denim dress and sandals. How long had she been there? Had she been eavesdropping?

"What's with all the ingredients you were talking about?" she asked. "Are you recording tomorrow?" Yep, she'd been listening in. How rude.

"Yes! Sana came up with more brilliant ideas for her sushi

creations. She's so creative and talented," Koji said, nearly bursting with excitement.

It wasn't lost on me that he'd said "more brilliant ideas." Like Harley knew about the video. Of course Koji told her about it. They spent time together.

"Cool," she said. "This is for that video that you were editing the other day? Can I join in?"

Koji turned to me. "It's up to Sana. Is that okay?"

Oh, great. Put it on me. If I said no, I'd look bad. I didn't want to say yes, either, though. So I shrugged.

"Fabulous," Harley exclaimed. She finally looked at me. "When are you recording the next episode?"

I sighed quietly. "Tomorrow."

"Great!" She put her hand on Koji's arm as she smiled at him. "Since you're the camera person, I'll be the director. And then we can both edit like we did the first episode."

I frowned. Koji and Harley had edited that first episode? Together?

"By the way," she said, taking out her phone. "Did you see the page-view counter?"

I had been so focused on the documentary and trying to cook

with Dad that I hadn't looked since I'd shown Alana and Liv on Sunday. I pulled out my phone, hit the app, and then gasped.

"Holy . . ." Koji said. His and Harley's heads were touching as they looked at her phone. Then he scooted over to me to point at my screen and nearly shouted in my ear, "Over one thousand views! Sana! You're a star!"

I stared down at my phone. How was this possible? All these strangers wanted to see me create kawaii creatures from rice? That was amazing! A grin burst onto my face and I glanced up at Koji, who was just inches away from me. My breath hitched as our eyes locked and he smiled down at me.

And then the spell was broken when Harley yanked on his arm. "We need to totally plan out the next episode. You don't want to tank and lose momentum." She said this as she caught my eye.

Koji nodded. "I'll get these ingredients together for tomorrow."

"That's great, thanks," I said, flashing a big smile at him, pointedly ignoring Harley. I didn't know why I got so prickly when she was around, but I did.

"What time are we filming?" Harley asked.

But Koji didn't seem to hear her. "So, Sana," he said, nudging me, "when can you come over?" Out of the corner of my eye

I saw Harley frown, and droop. I wanted to feel triumphant but instead I felt a little bad.

She sighed loudly, pushed her way between us, and walked straight into the house without a backward glance.

"How about noon?" I said, trying to forget the hurt look on Harley's face. "I'll eat an early lunch so we can get right to work."

"Sounds great," he said. "Can't wait!"

As I rode home, I pondered Harley's involvement. She was officially now part of this project and there was nothing I could do about it. I wished I'd told Koji I wanted to keep the video between us and that Harley would stop coming around, but, at the same time, I was filled with excitement. Our first video was getting attention. That meant more attention for the next one, and the next one.

A small voice in my head warned me I shouldn't do this. It could lead to trouble. But I squashed that voice. For the first time since I moved to Piper Bay, I had something to look forward to that was all mine.

# 19

"The star has arrived!" Koji announced as he let me into the house on Thursday. I took my shoes off and entered to see the kitchen transformed.

"Whoa," I said, jaw dropping despite wanting to play it cool in front of Harley. Not only was the kitchen different, but so was she. She smiled so brightly at me that I stumbled back against Koji. He caught me, his hands warm on my arms.

I expected Harley to glare at me, but instead she spun to the kitchen with her hands in the air like she was a fairy sprinkling wishing dust in the air.

"Koji and I worked on this all morning," she said.

Ah, that's why she was in such a good mood. She'd had him all to herself for hours already. Harley was wearing cream shortalls with a ribbed pink tank top. I was glad I'd worn a fitted white tee with the navy-blue skirt that Charli had left at my house the last time she'd slept over. It really didn't matter anyway since I'd be wearing an apron over my outfit the entire time.

I couldn't lie though, not even to myself. The kitchen setup was spectacular. Koji and Harley had cleared the kitchen of any distractions. They'd moved the canisters and knickknacks off the back counter. Koji had set up his phone on a selfie stick, which I knew stabilized video recordings. And everything I'd told Koji I would need for this recipe was laid out neatly.

"It's perfect," I said. Because it was.

Harley clapped her hands once. "Right! Let's get going. Sana, you stand over there. Koji, you're going to film from back here to get the best angle."

"Wait," I said. "Let's keep the same format as the first episode. Koji can record from above the counter and just show my hands and what I'm making."

Harley gave me an approving nod. "Good point. You're not the most important part of the video."

"That's not true at all," Koji said, moving next to me at the counter. "Sana *is* the show. She's the star and the creator. Without her, there are no adorable rice ball creatures."

I tilted my face up at Koji, who gazed at me. My cheeks got warm.

"Yeah, yeah," Harley said. "Got it. But Sana makes a good point. We don't want to veer off from our format now that we're establishing an audience."

I felt stuck. I didn't want to agree with Harley since she was only trying to shift the focus away from me, but I didn't want to argue with her because I couldn't risk showing my face on camera. It's not like my parents would ever come across the video, but what if Charli did?

Koji nudged me with his shoulder and rested against mine. "You're the star power, Sana. Whatever you say."

"I think it's better to focus on the food."

"Great," Harley shouted, making both me and Koji flinch. "Koji, get over here and start recording. We'll edit tonight and post. It's important not to let too much time go between episodes."

Wow. Harley had a very domineering personality. I missed the lightness and fun of recording with just Koji. This felt a lot more stressful. Harley acted like we were doing an assignment for a grade or something.

I arranged the ingredients in order of when I'd use them.

"Action!" Harley called.

Yeesh. "Today I'm making a flower sushi roll."

"Cut!"

I blinked at Harley. What was her deal?

"You're going to put people to sleep using that voice," Harley said. "Be expressive. Excited."

I scowled at her, but she wasn't fazed.

"Do you want people to watch the entire video or not?" Harley waved to Koji. "Take two, and action!"

Oh my god, I liked Harley better when she ignored me. I took a breath, trying to forget she was here and focus on why I was doing this. I mean, yeah, to see Koji, but mostly to be able to cook, to make dishes my way.

I started by putting a scoop of rice in a bowl and mixed it with beet juice to turn it pink for the flower petals. Using the bamboo mat, I shaped five skinny pink sushi rolls wrapped in nori. I narrated as I went, trying to make my voice upbeat by channeling the crafters from the videos Charli watched.

Once I got going, I really did forget about Harley, the camera, and even Koji as I got lost in making the flower I'd envisioned in my head. Once I wrapped the pink rolls around the cheese stick, I covered the entire thing in a thin layer of white rice with a large rectangle of nori, and rolled everything together with the bamboo mat. Slicing the roll revealed a perfect flower pattern in every piece.

"And cut!" Harley's voice startled me.

Koji detached the selfie stick from his phone and dashed over to my side. "Sana, these are amazing! Seriously!"

He leaned over the platter where I'd set up the flowers in a bouquet of sorts, his hair smelling like sunshine and grass. Koji snapped a few photos and then, with a mischievous grin, snapped a pic of me.

"Hey!" I said, patting my face to make sure I didn't have any grains of rice stuck to my cheeks.

"You look great," Koji said.

I couldn't help the smile that bloomed on my face. But the moment lasted all of two seconds before Harley swooped in between us, snagging the platter.

"Okay, let's see how these taste," Harley said, leading us to the table.

When we sat down, Harley scooted her chair closer to Koji,

who either didn't notice or didn't mind. She took a sushi roll, peeled the nori off the outside, and pinched a smidge of rice to pop in her mouth.

"Not bad," she said, her eyes on Koji. Not bad? She only ate a few grains of rice!

Koji had stuffed an entire flower roll into his mouth, making his cheeks bulge. He looked like an adorable chipmunk. That gave me a great idea for a future video: a chipmunk rice ball! As Koji chewed, I took a bite and was pleased with the good balance of flavors. The beet juice didn't interfere with the vinegary sushi rice, and the cheese actually tasted good with it. I'd been skeptical.

"This is goooood!" Koji said, picking up another sushi roll and shoving it into his mouth. This boy was a bottomless pit!

A look I couldn't decipher passed over Harley's face like a cloud. "I'm still hungry," she said. Well, of course! She hadn't eaten anything! "Let's go get some ice cream at our favorite place."

Koji looked over at me. "You game, Sana?"

Harley's lower lip stuck out in a pout. Did she really think Koji would just leave me out? She obviously didn't know him as well as she thought. Then again, she sure was comfortable coming and going at his house. I wondered how long they'd known each other. Did she live close? I had so many questions, and too many blanks to fill in. I needed to start getting some answers.

"Sure," I said. "But I need to clean up first."

"We'll help," Koji said.

Harley wrinkled her nose. Koji just laughed and nudged her, much like he'd nudged me earlier.

"Harley doesn't have to lift a finger at home," he explained.

She shrugged. "The benefit of having divorced parents. Parental guilt trumps everything. I don't have to do chores or study or go to summer camp. I get to do whatever I want all summer long."

Her parents were divorced. Maybe that's why she and Koji were close? They had that in common.

Harley stood up suddenly. "Ugh. My hands smell like vinegar. Be back in a sec!" She disappeared to the bathroom as Koji and I gathered the dishes. He washed and I dried.

"How long have you known Harley?" I asked.

"Since elementary school," he said, handing me a dish to dry.

"Does she go to your school? I know I haven't seen her around Piper Bay Middle."

Koji shook his head. "Her parents got divorced during sixth grade while I was in Los Angeles. She moved to Seattle with her mom. Harley stays here with her dad every summer and we hang out. It was nice to have her here when I got back last summer."

"So, you're best friends? Like me and Charli?" I asked. *Please don't be boyfriend and girlfriend.*

"Yeah, pretty much."

My heart filled with relief.

Koji continued. "When I lived in LA, she was the only one of my friends who kept in touch. And when I came back here and started at a private school, let's just say I had a hard time making friends. *Now* I have friends there, but most of them travel with their families in the summer, and unlike my sister, I don't drive, so it's harder to see them. They all live in Carmel. Anyway, Harley really made it easier for me when I returned home. She's always been there for me, no matter what."

Before I could process all that, Harley rejoined us and silently crept up super close behind Koji. I focused on drying the dishes, but I also felt a weird dark twinge thinking about how grateful he was to Harley. There was no doubt that they were very close.

"Where's this ice cream place?" I asked as I hung up my towel.

"On the other side of town," Koji said. "Harley's dad will drive us when he gets home in thirty minutes."

I glanced at the time. Nope, that wouldn't leave me enough time to get home before Mom. "I don't have that long," I said, unable to keep the disappointment out of my voice.

"Oh, that's too bad," Harley said brightly.

"I'll bring back a pint for you," Koji said. "What's your favorite flavor? You can have it tomorrow."

"Tomorrow?" Harley asked. "Dad and I are going to the aquarium tomorrow. You said you'd come, remember?"

Koji shook his head. "No, I said I'd think about it. I already promised to hang out with Sana tomorrow."

If looks could kill, I'd be a dead girl.

And suddenly, I didn't mind leaving Harley to get ice cream with Koji. Not when I'd have him all to myself tomorrow.

# 20

Koji and Harley sat close together on a bench outside the ice cream place. Koji smiled, his dimple making a deep pocket in his cheek, as he lifted their shared cone to Harley's mouth. She leaned forward, her eyes locked on his as she licked the cherry-pink scoop of ice cream. They gazed lovingly at one another.

"Sana, what's wrong with you?" Mom asked.

"What?" I startled out of my thoughts. I couldn't stop imagining Harley and Koji together.

"I asked you three times what you put in the ramen. It's really good." Mom nodded at her bowl.

"Oh, um, I added fresh miso and a little sesame oil to the soup base." I mentally shook the image of Harley and Koji out of my head.

"Are you okay?" Mom asked. "It must be hard with Charli away. Do you want me to get you a tutor to learn Japanese? It's probably hard to learn from recordings and workbooks. Plus it can't be healthy to spend so much time alone."

Ack! I'd forgotten I'd told Mom I was studying Japanese. No way did I want a tutor. That would interfere with my cooking lessons, and seeing Koji.

I took a deep breath. "Actually I've been hanging out with this girl, Harley." That was the truth.

"Oh! Is that why you've been spending so much time out of the house?" Mom asked. "Why don't you bring her by sometime?"

Oh. No. "I'll see," I said, trying not to make Mom suspicious. "She's busy all weekend with her dad." A half-truth was better than an outright lie, right?

"What will you do tomorrow, then?"

"Mom," I said, not bothering to keep the impatience out of my voice. "I'm not a little kid. I can entertain myself. I don't need company every second of every day."

Mom raised her eyebrows at me. "You don't have to get upset, Sana. You and Charli are always together, so I was worried about you. That's all."

"Sorry. I do miss Charli. But I'm okay, Mom. I promise."

She shook her head with a rueful smile. "So this is you going through your rebellious stage? I guess I can handle it."

Guilt dripped through me. I spent the afternoon trying to be the good daughter Mom knew and watched a movie with her. After that I holed up in my room with a notebook to scribble down ideas for kawaii sushi. Maybe tomorrow Koji and I could record without movie director Harley around. Maybe we could go back to just having fun.

Just then, my phone pinged.

**Koji:**
New episode is up. LMK what you think!

I immediately opened my laptop and clicked the link, my heart pounding. As the video started, music played over the title screen. It was a little different from the original version—it had the same font but now with kawaii sushi scattered around the border. Koji's voice-over introducing the episode made my heart sizzle like garlic dropped in butter on a hot pan.

Then there I was. Well, at least there my hands were. My voice sounded pretty good, not shaky or squeaky, and I had to admit grudgingly that Harley's direction for me to sound more upbeat had been helpful. I sounded happy and passionate. All in all it wasn't bad. The page-view counter was already at thirty, with twenty thumbs-up. I clicked to make it twenty-one.

My phone rang, startling me. It was Koji. Calling me! I nearly dropped the phone in my haste to answer it.

"Hello? Hi!" I nearly shouted. I had to remind myself to breathe. "Hey," I said a little more casually, but then I realized I'd basically said hi three times in a row.

"Hey! Sorry, I couldn't wait anymore. What did you think?"

"It's great!" I exclaimed. "And the addition of music at the opening and closing is perfect."

"I thought so, too," Koji said. "Harley picked it. We spent most of the rest of the day editing it."

The movie in my head of Harley and Koji sharing an ice cream cone was replaced by one of the two of them in his darkened room, sitting side by side at his computer, romantic music playing in the background.

"Hello? Sana? You still there?"

I looked at the counter. The views were now up to forty-two. I checked the first episode and the counter was in the two thousands. Wow! "I wonder who all is watching our videos?"

I heard Koji tapping on his keyboard. "No idea, but that's pretty awesome. We should record another. Tomorrow okay?"

Without Harley? "For sure," I said.

The first thing I did after ending the call was text all my friends the link. Well, all my friends except for Charli. That made me sad. I wanted to be able to share this with her.

**Esme:**
Sana! This is awesome!

**Liv:**
You're a star!

**Alana:**
Yum! Tho seriously Sana you should show your face.

**Sana:**
Thanks. Woohoo!
And no way on showing my face!

**Esme:**
Nice editing work, too. You?

**Sana:**
Nope.

I filled them in.

**Esme:**
You need to keep her away from your
man. She sounds like trouble.

**Sana:**
Koji is not my man.

**Esme:**
You're right about that if you don't
get her away from him!

**Alana:**
Es, be gentle with our Sana.

**Sana:**
It's nothing.

**Esme:**
Befriend her! Keep your enemies close!

**Sana:**
I gotta go. xoxo

I didn't want Esme and the others to wind me up. I hated
the twinges of jealousy I felt every time I thought of Harley and
Koji together. They had a long history. I'd only just met him. I
couldn't compete with that.

Could I?

# 21

The next morning, I woke up giddy. I was spending the afternoon with Koji, without Harley. I grabbed my phone off my nightstand and went straight to our video. And almost dropped my phone, staring at the counter. Over one thousand views overnight! As I watched, the counter ticked up ten more views.

And I had over fifty missed texts from my San Francisco friends. Mostly of them gasping and squealing and cheering as the counter went up.

**Alana:**
It's happening! You're actually going viral!

I shook my head. Even if the video didn't go viral, that was over two thousand people who watched me making kawaii omusubi.

My phone buzzed and my heart stuttered when I saw it was

Koji. Who needed to do cardio workouts when I could get the same reaction by checking my phone?

**Koji:**
Did you see?

**Sana:**
YES! 1000+!

**Koji:**
I'm going to make a teaser video
using the bunny clip from that
recording we did for your cousin.

**Sana:**
Don't use my name or show my face, okay?

The dots appeared, but then they disappeared. And reappeared. I wiped sweaty palms on my shirt. Was he going to question my request? Could I trust he wouldn't go ahead and just use the clip as is?

My screen finally lit up with his response.

**Koji:**
No worries! I'm an expert editor!

I was relieved to read that, but also wondered why it had taken him so long to type that.

**Sana:**
Thanks!

**Koji:**
Can you get here soon? Now?

**Sana:**
I'll be there in 30!

**Koji:**
Seconds? Great!

I grinned all the way to Koji's, but then sobered. The longer I kept what I was doing from Charli, the harder it would be to tell her. So I needed to find out the truth about Koji's past once and for all. If I could prove to her that he wasn't a horrible or dangerous person, I could tell her about the videos. And hopefully she wouldn't be angry at me for sneaking around with Koji.

Right. I'd get that over with before we started to record.

When I got to Koji's, I was a little overwhelmed. The counter was crammed with bowls and bags of almost everything from their pantry and fridge.

"I won't need all that," I said, laughing. "Let's do the panda I never got to make."

As Koji and I put back all the ingredients I wouldn't need, I took a deep breath to steady my nerves. "Hey, so I have a question," I said.

"Yeah?"

*Just get it over with*, I told myself as I let the words spill out. "Why did you move to LA?"

Koji put the container of tofu back down onto the counter. "Because my mom thought I needed a male role model. I lived with my uncle for a year."

I nodded. "Yes, I remember you telling me that, but why did she think you needed a role model?"

The light dimmed in Koji's eyes, like a cloud passing over the sun. I instantly regretted pushing. But then again, if we were friends, we should be able to share with each other. I waited the seconds it took for Koji to answer.

But instead, he had a question of his own. "Why don't you want your name or face on camera for these videos?"

Right. So maybe we weren't the kind of friends who shared everything yet.

"Sana?" Koji prompted.

How did he flip the tables so smoothly? Now I was the one trying to deflect!

I shrugged. "I just don't feel comfortable in the spotlight," I said.

It wasn't entirely a lie, but I knew it wasn't the truth either. Still, there was no way I was telling him about my dad. And I didn't want Koji to keep digging. Time to change the topic.

"We should record," I said.

"Let's do it!" Koji took his station at his phone, adjusting it so it was right over my hands.

I felt the tension melt off me with the familiarity of our movements.

"Okay," I said. "Ready!"

"Action!" Koji's voice was much less jarring than Harley's, that was for sure. And in seconds I got lost in shaping an adorable panda face. I kept up a steady chatter, describing what I was doing, and before I knew it, the pandas were done.

"And cut!" Koji tapped his phone and brought it over to the counter, once again snapping photos of the finished products. And this time he gave me a warning. "Heads up, Chef. I'm snapping a pic!"

All the weirdness from our conversation before disappeared and Koji and I were back to our normal comfortable, happy selves. I smiled for the camera, and then my grin grew bigger as Koji leaned next to me for a selfie.

"Can I have a copy of those?" I asked, even though I really only wanted the one of the two of us together.

"Sure!" He tapped and a second later my phone buzzed with the photos.

I glanced at the one of us together. We looked cute! I couldn't wait to share it with my friends.

Koji raised the plate of omusubi. I'd created five chubby pandas and three that were only panda faces, using rice and nori. "These are amazing, Sana," Koji said, bumping me with his shoulder. "You're a cook and an artist rolled into one."

I admired my work. Not bad at all. Even Charli would probably rave about these. I really wished I could share them with her. Maybe I'd try to talk to her about Koji tomorrow during our scheduled call. I didn't really need to know what happened, did I? All that really mattered was who he was now. Although I hoped at some point he would trust me enough to tell me the story.

"Hungry?" I asked. Even though I'd only met Koji a little over two weeks ago, I knew the answer. He grinned and took the plate over to the table.

"Hey, why didn't you call me for lunch?" Yuri slid into her seat at the table. She grabbed two panda omusubi and started to eat.

"Geez, Mom would flip at your lack of manners," Koji complained. He snapped up pandas like he was afraid we'd run out.

Yuri caught my eye. "Thank you, Sana, for this delicious and adorable food."

"You're welcome, but once again, all this is yours anyway."

"Nice videos, by the way," Yuri said to me. "You've got a lot of views," she said, chewing. "You can thank me because I shared it with my friends, who shared with their friends. And now I'm pretty sure most of those views are people we don't know personally."

"I was wondering how it caught on so quickly," Koji said. "Thanks!"

I started to clean up. It was nice not having Harley around. Even though I'd had fun with Koji, I knew that he and Harley had a much closer relationship. They'd known each other for years. So as much as I liked Koji, I had to remind myself that he treated me and Harley the same. He touched her, or rather nudged her, as often as he did me. And in fact, he'd put his arm around her at least once that I'd seen. Harley probably snuggled up with him on the couch to watch their "favorite show," whatever it was. She'd lean on his shoulder and he'd rest his cheek against her head as they laughed together. Maybe I should just give up on my little crush.

"Sana?" Koji's voice interrupted my thoughts.

Yuri had left and Koji had snuck up beside me.

"I think that plate is clean," he said with a teasing tone.

I looked down at the dish I'd probably been scrubbing the whole time I was lost in thought, and my cheeks got hot.

Koji gently nudged me over. "I'll wash. You already did a ton of work."

And with that one bit of contact, all my resolve melted away. I liked him. I really liked him. And even if I had to deal with Harley, I didn't want to give up time with Koji. I wasn't going anywhere.

# 22

"Lemonade?" Koji asked once we were done cleaning up.

"Yes, please."

As soon as we sat down in the backyard, Koji said, "Oh, and while you were washing that one dish," he flashed me a teasing smile, "I uploaded the teaser clip."

I set my glass on the ground and brought the video up on my phone. He'd made a short clip telling people that more kawaii sushi videos were on the way. He'd done a great job editing out my face and the audio where we were using our names. Impressive!

"This is great," I said.

I tucked my phone back in my pocket and sipped my drink. Koji's lemonade was the best. He'd even added a sprig of fresh mint.

"See anything new?" he asked.

I looked out over his garden at the lush leaves on the cucumber plant and the spiky rosemary bush and some small green fruit that hadn't been there a week ago. "You have tomatoes!" The first thing I thought of was how I might be able to incorporate them once they ripened.

"Yeah, for sure, but no, something else."

I squinted as I looked around again, wondering if he was testing me. "Um . . . what should I be seeing?"

Koji pointed to my left. There, in a large blue-and-white ceramic planter, was a hibiscus plant bursting with crimson blooms. How had I missed that?

"Oooh!" I cooed. "Hibiscus are my favorite flower!"

"I know. You said that the first time we sat here."

"You remembered?" I asked.

"Of course!"

Koji only ever planted things that provided food—fruits, vegetables, herbs. He said he didn't plant flowers. Had he planted these for . . . me?

"Here!" Koji leapt up and pulled clippers from a box. He neatly snipped off a stem and handed it to me. Our fingers touched as I took the hibiscus from him. I twirled it as a smile blossomed on my face.

"Don't move," he said, and he snapped a pic.

Inside I was melting into a big puddle of molten chocolate. This was like a scene out of one of Alana's favorite romantic comedies.

Koji looked at his screen and smiled. "Perfect."

I blushed even more if that was possible, and tucked the bloom behind my ear. The first thing I'd do when I got home was press and save this forever. Fortunately I'd done a flower-pressing craft with Charli a few months ago.

We sipped our lemonades as a blue jay scolded us from the lemon tree. Maybe he wanted some lemonade, too. Usually I was comfortable with silence, particularly when eating or drinking, but right now I was buzzing with energy.

"Do you think—" I said at the same time Koji said, "So I was thinking—"

We both stopped talking and laughed.

"You first," Koji said.

"Oh, I was just wondering if maybe your mom might let

us use the stove the next time we record. I want to incorporate omurice in our videos. Maybe put the omelet on the bottom like a canvas and use food items to make pictures on top, like a garden with butterflies and ladybugs."

"Love it! Mom will be fine with that. She's home on Thursday anyway."

"Okay, great!"

Harley would probably be around. Or maybe she would go away on a long vacation with her dad. Nah, that was just wishful thinking. If only I could be as close to him as Harley was—close enough to just drop by and hang out to watch TV or whatever.

Koji shifted and his chair scraped against the concrete as he scooted closer to me. My breath hitched as Koji reached out and placed his hand over mine. I gripped the arm of my chair so tightly that I was losing feeling in my fingers. I really, really wanted to play it cool, so I slowly eased my death grip, but the minute Koji felt my hand move, he pulled away.

When I looked up at him, he shrugged. "Sorry."

"No! Don't apologize. That was nice."

"Really?"

I nodded, wishing I didn't blush so easily. I flipped my palm up and peeked at Koji through my hair. He reached over and we interlocked fingers. Now we were holding hands for real. I was holding hands with a cute boy! We smiled goofily at each other. I felt like this was a moment—a pivotal moment I would never ever forget. A boy planted my favorite flower for me, and then gave me a clipped blossom. And now we were holding hands! *Please don't let anything ruin today,* I prayed.

"So," Koji said. "All we've been doing is cooking and filming."

Oh no. Was he going to suggest quitting? Maybe he was tired of watching me cook. Or bored doing all that recording and editing. Panic rose inside me like a soup pot boiling over. I wanted to keep spending time with Koji, for sure, but also, I really loved making those videos.

"We should get a reward for all our hard work," Koji said.

"A reward?"

"Yeah, like that saying, all work and no play or something like that."

Oh. Was recording our videos work?

"I'm totally having a blast doing our show," he said quickly. "I just meant, maybe we could do something else. Too. Also. Together."

The faintest blush spread across his cheeks.

"Sure," I said. "That sounds like fun."

Adorable Koji looked both relieved and happy. "Great! So, what do you like to do? I mean, other than cook?"

My mind went blank. I realized that basically all I did was watch crafting videos and do art projects with Charli. When had my life become so narrow? Back in San Francisco, my friends and I used to go to museums and hike and collect stones on the beach.

Like he'd been listening in on my thoughts, Koji asked, "Do you like the beach?"

"Yes."

"Cool. Let's do that!"

"But how will we get there?" Piper Bay was a misleading name. There was no bay and we weren't close enough to any beach to bike there.

"Yuri can drive us," Koji said. "If you don't mind."

"That would be awesome," I said. "I like your sister."

"She has friends in Carmel, so she can drop us off and go hang with them. I have a favorite beach we can go to. Well, it's really more a cove. We can pack a bento."

My heart was flapping all over the place. Seriously! This day was the best. My first date. With Koji!

"Can you go on Sunday?" Koji asked. "I mean, if you don't have plans for the holiday weekend."

The Fourth of July wasn't until Tuesday, but family celebrations were nonexistent at my house. The restaurant came first even when it was closed. Dad was always working on something. Last year, I'd joined Mom, Uncle Luke, and Charli for an orchestra concert in the park and a picnic, but I'd begged off this year. Without Charli, it wouldn't be fun.

Mom was home on Sundays, but I didn't hesitate. "That would be great! Thanks!"

I didn't know how I was going to get away for a full day, but nothing was going to stop me from my first date ever.

# 23

We were so focused on grinning at each other, our hands still interlocked, that we didn't hear the squeak of the back gate or footsteps behind us until Harley's voice made us both jump.

"Hey," she said, walking around our chairs to stand in front of us.

I wasn't sure who released the other's hand first, but suddenly mine felt cold and empty.

"Hey!" Koji said, grinning at Harley like he was truly happy to see her. "I thought you were going to be gone till after dinner. Didn't you and your dad go to that clam chowder place?"

"The Fish Hopper," Harley said. "Yeah, we went for a late lunch and just got home."

"Cool! Sana and I recorded another video. You want to edit later?" Koji asked.

I felt like I'd been dunked in an ice bath watching Koji smile at Harley like that, inviting her to edit *our* show.

Harley flipped her hair over her shoulder. "Definitely."

Koji stood up. "Sit."

She flashed me a triumphant grin and pointedly moved her chair away from mine. At least she'd noticed Koji and I had been sitting very close together. "What are you up to?" she asked, all casual.

"Not much, just chilling," Koji said, tucking his hands in his jeans pockets while rocking back on his heels.

"Cool. What do you want to do this weekend?" Harley kept her eyes on Koji, making it very obvious I was not part of this conversation. "I have to do more dad-and-daughter stuff tomorrow, but I'm free Sunday."

Koji shook his head. "Sana and I are going to the beach on Sunday."

I tensed, worried that Koji would invite her along. But he'd made it sound like it would just be us. He wouldn't invite someone else on our date. Would he?

"Oh?" Harley asked, smiling, but her smile definitely did not reach her eyes.

"Yep." Koji nodded.

There was a long beat, a perfect opening for Koji to invite Harley. I nibbled my bottom lip.

But Koji just cleared his throat and asked, "Do you want a lemonade?"

It would have been hard to miss the disappointment that flickered over Harley's face. If Koji noticed, he didn't react. I felt kind of bad for her. Although it was obvious to me how Harley felt about Koji, he was either clueless or chose to ignore it.

As soon as he went into the house, Harley turned to me, giving me an overly sweet smile that I didn't trust one bit. "So what beach are you going to?" she asked.

My radar went up, like Charli's *danger danger* signal.

"I don't know yet." I was glad Koji hadn't told me because I was pretty sure Harley was going to try to crash.

"I wonder if it's that cove Koji likes?" Harley leaned back in her chair, tilting her face up to the sun. "We've gone there together, just the two of us. A lot."

I forced my face to remain neutral. She was just trying to get to me. And even if he had taken Harley there, even if it had been a date, he was taking me now. He had invited *me*. Or maybe she was trying to tell me our plans weren't anything special. That he was only being nice because we were friends. But he'd held my hand and given me a flower. I reached up to touch it. Friends didn't do that. Did they?

Harley's eyes followed the movement of my hand. Then she noticed the planter just as Koji returned with Harley's lemonade.

"Is that new?" she asked, jutting her chin to the hibiscus plant.

"Yeah!" Koji said. "I've been working with a lot of flowers at my job, so I decided to give them a try."

"Koji doesn't like people to touch his plants," Harley said softly to me.

"Harley, it's okay," Koji said quickly, his voice sounding a bit like a warning. "*I* cut the flower."

Harley narrowed her eyes at me, but it didn't faze me. I was glowing, hearing Koji speak up like that. Like he wasn't going to let Harley make me feel uncomfortable.

"A little help?" Mrs. Yamada's voice came from the gate.

We all jumped up to help her with the bags of groceries she was lugging, although I noticed Harley was a beat slower and ended up without anything to carry.

Mrs. Yamada and Koji led the way into the house, but before

I could step in to follow, Harley's hot breath blasted into my ear.

"Don't get too comfortable," she said in a low voice. "You think Koji likes you, but he's a flirt. He likes the attention he gets from girls, but he gets bored pretty quick. You're not as special as you think."

I shrugged to hide the pounding of my heart, like it didn't matter to me. I helped Mrs. Yamada and Koji put away the groceries while Harley disappeared down the hallway.

"I have to get going," I said as I put away the last can into the pantry.

"Okay, dear," Mrs. Yamada said. "But I'm looking forward to Wednesday."

That made the heaviness I felt lighten just a little.

"Hey," Koji said, "give me your address. Yuri and I will pick you up on Sunday."

I hoped the panic didn't show on my face. "Oh, it's okay. I don't mind coming here. What time is good?"

Fortunately Mrs. Yamada had already left the room. I didn't want to remind her that she hadn't met my parents. As I suspected, Koji didn't really care.

"Okay," he said. "How about eleven?"

"I'll be here. And I'll bring the bento."

"Really? No. That doesn't seem right. I mean, I invited you."

I raised my eyebrows at him and gave him a coy look Esme would have been proud of. "You don't want my bento?"

He laughed. "Fine, yes, I do! Make the lunch, I'll bring dessert."

Koji walked me to the door. "Harley and I will edit today's video and I'll upload it tomorrow afternoon. Sound good?"

"Sure."

Just as I was stepping out, I saw Harley watching us from the living room with a look on her face that made me shiver. Like she was plotting and planning. But I knew no matter what Harley said, Koji wouldn't back out on a commitment. Harley was jealous, and while I could sympathize a little, I left feeling secure that Koji liked me.

Sunday couldn't come soon enough.

# 24

Saturday morning, I woke up in time for a video call with Charli. We'd planned to talk early because even her weekends were jam-packed with activities and classes.

"Hey, sleepyhead," Charli said, immediately noticing I was still in bed and in my pj's.

"You're the one who complained about waking up too early at the start of summer," I reminded her.

She grinned. "It's different here! There's so much I want to soak up from this program. I can't believe we're already a week in. It's going by too quickly!"

"Quick for you," I grumbled. "I miss you!" While I was having fun with Koji, I really did miss my cousin. And I hated that I was keeping a big part of my life from her.

"I miss you, too! Okay, I've been talking way too much about myself. What are you up to?"

"I'll be helping Mom with her home renovation project starting Monday," I groaned.

Charli nodded. "Dad told me how Auntie Lucy is really getting into decorating. So awesome!"

I smiled because I was happy for my mom.

"Are you working on *your* big project? Have you come up with any ideas to convince Uncle Hiro to teach you to cook again?"

"Yes."

There was a brief pause and Charli cocked her head at me with a grin. "You're up to something! What? Spill!"

Should I tell her? Could I risk it? Maybe I could convince her that Koji wasn't a bad influence now that I'd gotten to know him. Except, something told me I'd just upset her.

"Sana?"

"Oh, yeah. I think I have a plan, but I'm not ready to share it yet." Vague, but not a lie at least.

"You're keeping secrets? Oooh, Sana it must be a *serious* plan. Promise you'll tell me soon!"

I nodded, changing the subject to ask about her roommate's pottery. Then Charli told me about this other girl who was a genius with a camera. After twenty minutes I felt like I knew everyone in her program and all the teachers.

"Okay, I have to go!" Charli said finally. "We have a field trip to a local block-print museum. I'm excited!"

Before I could sign off, Charli ended the call. It was nice to see her so happy and going after the things that mattered to her. I really wished I could share with her the ways I was doing that, too.

I headed downstairs to find Mom sitting on the couch, perusing catalogs.

"Sana! You're up earlier than usual. Come sit. After I'm done with the half bath, I figured we could start in on the kitchen."

That got my attention. "It would be awesome to update it!"

She smiled at me. "I knew you'd like that. The landlord has a pretty tight budget, so we need to be creative."

I flopped down next to Mom and picked up a kitchen decorating magazine. And as I flipped through the pages, I envisioned a perfect kitchen where Dad and I would cook together.

"Hey, Mom?"

"Hmmm?"

"Can I make dinner tonight?"

Mom beamed at me. "That would be wonderful. Thank you, Sana."

At least that was one benefit to having Dad away at the restaurant—free rein in the kitchen to practice my skills! I could still come up with something fabulous to wow him!

I leapt up from the couch and rummaged through the pantry, pulling out ingredients. Then I peeked in the fridge.

"Do we have ground pork?" I asked.

Mom looked up from her magazine. "I'll get some at the market today. Do you need anything else?"

I looked in the freezer. "Gyoza wrappers."

Mom broke into a huge smile. "I love gyoza!"

"I know that, Mom," I laughed. She loved all Japanese food, but especially the dishes her mom used to make. The kinds of food Dad used to prepare before he became a big-time superstar sushi chef.

"Good thing Dad won't be home," I said.

"Why do you say that?" Mom closed the magazine.

I shrugged. "Because he'd take over. And he'd *never* make dumplings."

"That's not true at all, Sana. Where do you get such outrageous ideas? Dad loves gyoza."

Whatever. Mom was clueless when it came to Dad, that much was obvious.

She stood and stretched. "I'm going to shower, and then I'm off to look at some kitchen countertops. Do you want to come with me?"

"Sure!" It turned out I liked renovation if it was our kitchen.

"We can stop at your favorite boba tea shop on the way back," Mom said. "A fun mother-daughter day!"

"Hey, by the way," I said, realizing how I could use this moment to my advantage. "I'm going to hang out with my friend tomorrow all day. Is that okay?"

"Why don't you bring her over so I can meet her?"

"I will. Another time. My friend's sister is taking us to a beach in Carmel."

A concerned look crossed her face. "Her sister is driving? How old is she?"

"She's going to be a senior."

"I really would feel better if I could meet her."

"Mom, you said you trust me. It's only to Carmel. I'll text

you when we leave, when we get there, and when we're on our way home."

I held my breath as Mom contemplated.

"Okay, but please bring her over this week. I like to know your friends."

Whew! I didn't answer, but Mom didn't seem to notice.

While Mom was in the shower, I checked our YouTube site, but Koji hadn't uploaded the video yet. The views for the first two videos and the teaser combined were over four thousand! I was so excited. Maybe I could be one of those celebrity chefs when I got older. Or why wait? Once *This Is How I Roll* went viral, I could be the first celebrity kid chef. I'd be invited onto all the talk shows. Baxton would do a documentary on *me*. And then Dad would be the one wanting to work with me. I let myself fall into a full-blown fantasy that made me feel on top of the world.

But the fantasy was just that . . . a dream that hadn't come true yet. I glanced at my phone again, wondering how many views our newest episode would get. And that made me think about Koji and Harley editing together.

It was obvious to me how Harley felt about Koji, but did he

know? And the bigger question was, how did Koji feel about Harley compared to how he felt about me? He treated us almost the same, except he spent a lot more time with her. But then again, he'd planted my favorite flower and gave me one. He'd held my hand. He was taking me on a date to his favorite beach.

I was grateful to have the distraction of shopping for back-splash tiles and countertops with Mom. She agreed that an assortment of glass tiles in blues that mimicked the ocean was a great idea. Our tight budget meant we couldn't get the marble countertops I wanted. But Mom found a good substitute in laminate that looked nice at least. Anything would look better than the apricot tiles that were in our kitchen right now. To save money, we decided to paint the kitchen cabinets white rather than replace them.

When we got home, it was almost time for me to start dinner. Mom ran to the market for my ingredients and I checked my phone, but Koji still hadn't uploaded our latest video.

To kill time, I hopped on my bike and rode to Dad's. When I walked in the back door, Ethan and Manny were prepping for tonight's omakase dinner.

"Hey, Sana, long time no see!" Manny said.

"Sana!" Ethan called. "How's my favorite sous-chef?"

One time, Mom's car had gotten a flat tire in Carmel and Dad had to drive out to get her. I'd stopped by the restaurant and Ethan had let me help with prep until Manny arrived for his shift. I'd been there and gone by the time Dad had returned, but that had been one of the best moments in my life since moving to Piper Bay.

After making sure that Dad wasn't in the tiny kitchen, I walked over to the pantry area, squeezing between Ethan, who was expertly skinning fish, and Manny, who was roasting nori. The major prep happened behind the scenes, but when the doors opened, all the sushi was made at the bar in front of the customers. It was a tight fit here in the kitchen, but I was careful not to get in the way. My eyes skimmed the shelf for the craft-brewed shoyu I loved. Before taking it, I made sure there was another full bottle behind it, which there was.

"Cooking something special?" Ethan asked.

"Gyoza for my mom," I said. "I want to make a dipping sauce."

"You're cooking?" Dad asked as he walked into the kitchen. It was already a small space with three of us crammed into it, but with Dad here, too, suddenly it felt hard to breathe.

"I won't make a mess, and I'll clean up right after and put everything back exactly where it goes. You won't even know I was there," I said in a rush.

Ethan and Manny burst out laughing and fist-bumped each other. "Oh, looks like Chef Hiro is just as strict at home as he is in the restaurant kitchen."

Dad actually grinned with a sheepish duck of the head. Then his face turned stern when he noticed what was in my hand. "Are you stealing from my kitchen, Susannah?"

I blinked at him dramatically, hoping I looked adorable.

"Go," Dad said gruffly. "And I will be checking the kitchen when I get home tonight."

"Thanks, Dad!" As I scooted past him, he ruffled my hair. I felt light all the way home. Maybe he didn't mind me cooking at home after all. Or maybe he just didn't want to lose face in front of his staff. It didn't matter. I was cooking dinner tonight! And nothing was going to ruin it!

# 25

In between chopping and mixing, I kept checking for the new video, but by five o'clock Koji still hadn't posted it. I hoped he was okay.

"Oh, that looks good," Mom said, peering over the counter.

"Shoo," I said with a grin. "I'll call you when dinner is ready."

Mom gave me a thumbs-up and returned to the living room to her catalogs. She was much happier these days focusing on the house reno. It made me double my determination to convince Dad to let me cook with him again. Dreams were important and I was going to make sure my family supported mine.

After mixing the seasoned ground pork with diced shallots and fresh ginger, I made the dumplings. Using a teaspoon, I measured out the pork mixture and folded it into the gyoza wrappers, pinching the dough closed the way Grandma had shown me before she died three years earlier.

I snapped a photo of my gyoza and texted it to Koji.

**Sana:**
Getting ready to cook!

The read notification showed up immediately and I sat there, smiling, waiting for his response. But it didn't come. Wow. He must be super busy. In fact, I realized that today was the first day in a week he hadn't texted me.

"Is it time to eat yet?" Mom called. "I'm hungry."

I laughed as I took out the big cast-iron pan, using both hands to lug it to the stove top. After I turned on the gas burner, I oiled the pan and carefully arranged the gyoza in a tight circular pattern. The dumplings sizzled and popped as they fried, and I quickly put together a cornstarch slurry, pouring the mixture into the pan to make a web that would connect the gyoza in a beautiful design. Next I covered the pan with a large platter to finish them off by steaming them. And finally I put together my special dipping sauce, tasting as I went. Not bad at all!

It was then I realized I couldn't finish dinner without help after all. There was no way I could flip that cast-iron pan by myself to plate the gyoza. Could I lift them out of the pan with two large spatulas? No, they'd probably break apart. Dad would have scolded me for not thinking through all the steps ahead of time. I shook my head. I felt disappointment in myself that was just as heavy as Dad's would have been. I fretted for a minute longer, knowing the longer I waited, the bigger the possibility I would burn dinner.

"Mom?!"

She ran into the room, panic on her face. "Are you okay? Did you hurt yourself?" she shouted in Japanese.

"No! I'm fine." I said quickly. "I just need your help flipping the pan."

She put a hand to her chest. "You scared me!"

"Sorry."

Even though Mom happily helped me flip the fried gyoza onto the plate and they looked gorgeous in the pattern I'd made, I felt like I'd failed. I hadn't managed to cook gyoza all on my own after all.

While Mom set the table and poured hot water for herself and cold for me, I checked my phone quickly, but there was nothing from Koji and no video yet. After ladling my dipping sauce into shallow blue bowls, I placed the platter of gyoza in the center of the table. They looked really good.

"These are amazing," Mom said, smiling proudly at me. "Even better than Dad's!"

I buzzed with warmth as Mom kept raving.

"You created this dipping sauce?" When I nodded, Mom said, "You're going to have to share this with Dad. I'll bet he could use it with one of his sushi dishes."

Yeah. Right. That was never going to happen.

Mom gobbled up the lightly salted chilled watermelon cubes I served for dessert. She offered to do the dishes, but I insisted. I'd told Dad I would do all the cleanup and put everything away. Mom wouldn't be as careful. I didn't want to take any chances and have Dad forbid me from our home kitchen.

"Movie after you're done?" Mom asked.

"Sure!"

I cleaned up and double-checked everything, ensuring Dad wouldn't be disappointed, then glanced at my phone. My heart tripped down my ribs when I saw I had a text message from Koji. Finally!

**Koji:**
Never mind about tomorrow. Don't
come back to my house. Ever.

# 26

By the time the sun rose on Sunday—the day I thought my dreams would come true—I was still in bed wearing yesterday's clothes. I might have slept a little, but mostly I'd lain awake with my mind spinning out of control.

I'd texted Koji at least ten times last night, but he hadn't responded at all. In fact, after the first "read" notification, my others hadn't been opened. Or he'd blocked me. I sat up, rubbing my eyes, and grabbed my phone from my pillow. Still nothing. I stumbled to my laptop and checked YouTube. He hadn't posted our newest video, but he hadn't deleted the others, at least.

I stared out the window at our brown patch of lawn. It reminded me of Koji and his part-time job and how we should probably put in drought-resistant plants and water with our leftover dishwater. My heart felt heavy in my chest, like a huge stone was sitting on it.

What had happened? Charli's warning echoed in my head. Could Koji not be who I thought he was?

The only explanation I could think of was that Harley interfered. Something had happened, all right. Harley had happened.

The more I thought about it, the angrier I felt. What right did she have to come between me and Koji, even if she was jealous!

Koji didn't *seem* like the fickle type. But then I remembered Harley's warning. That he was a flirt and got tired of girls easily. That really didn't seem like him. Neither did the curt message he'd sent.

There was only one way to find out the truth.

When I knocked on Koji's back door, Mrs. Yamada answered with a smile. "Sana! It's good to see you." She waved me in and as I took off my shoes, she called out, "Koji! Sana's here!"

My heart hammering, I followed her into the kitchen, where she was putting away groceries. I helped her since by now I knew where everything went.

"How goes the cooking show?" Mrs. Yamada asked, handing

me a package of soba. "I love what the two of you are doing. Your creations are so clever!"

"Thanks," I said, putting the soba in the pantry with the pasta. Her kitchen was just as organized as Dad's.

"I'm looking forward to cooking with you this week," Mrs. Yamada said. That made me happy. Even if Koji didn't take me to the beach today, even if I couldn't somehow convince him that Harley had it out for me, at least I still had my cooking lessons.

"Where is that boy?" Mrs. Yamada wondered. We'd finished putting away the groceries. I realized with a sinking heart that he was avoiding me. "He might have his headphones on," she said. "I'll go get him."

"I'll wait in the yard," I said. Whatever happened, I was pretty sure I didn't want to have Mrs. Yamada overhear. I was definitely getting a very bad vibe.

Gazing at the garden in my usual chair, I thought about the times I'd sat here with Koji talking about cooking and gardening, sipping his lemonade, and making plans for our show. I gripped the armrest, remembering how just two days ago he'd given me a flower, held my hand, and asked me out.

I was going to get to the bottom of this and fix it. I deserved an explanation, not to be ghosted by someone I'd thought was a friend.

Finally, I heard the back door open. Koji appeared in front of me. He didn't sit down. Somehow he managed to make navy-blue sweatpants and an oversize plain white tee look good. As I stood up to face him, his eyes sparked with anger. It made no sense.

"What's going on?" I asked. "Why are you mad at me?"

"You tell me." Koji's voice was flat and hard, like a stone. It was a voice I didn't recognize at all. The voice of a stranger. A chill crept up my spine, freezing me in place. Was this the Koji Charli had warned me about?

"I don't know what you mean," I said, frowning. "You're the one bailing on me."

"I may be bailing, but you're the liar."

My heart slammed into my chest hard, shattering the ice that had been holding me in place. "What?"

"Don't." Koji crossed his arms so tight his biceps bulged. "I can't believe anything you say. Not anymore. Just leave and don't come back."

I blinked, speechless. He was ice-cold. Not at all the warm, friendly, funny Koji I'd been hanging out with.

He took a step back, like being close to me disgusted him. "And don't even think about cooking with my mom. I haven't told her who you really are, but I will if you come back. I don't want to hurt her, but I don't want you to either. Just tell her you can't come by anymore and stay away."

I blinked again, trying hard to keep the angry tears from spilling over. "I would never hurt your mom!"

"No? Then why have you lied about who you are?"

I opened my mouth, but no words came out.

"When Harley told me, I didn't believe her. I defended you! But then I checked it out and everything Harley said was true. Your last name is Mikami. Your dad is the owner and chef of Mikami Sushi. There's going to be a freakin' documentary about him like he's some super wonderful person, when he's a rich, vain narcissist who puts people out of business!"

Suddenly any shame at being caught in my lie was overtaken by fury. "You have no right to talk about my dad like that! You don't know him!"

"Well, I don't know you either," Koji said calmly. "And I don't want to know you. Go away, Sana. And don't ever come back."

As he stormed back to the house, the tears I'd been holding back slid down my face. I ran to my bike and pedaled home.

It was over. Everything was over.

# 27

I was humiliated, angry, and hurt. All those emotions swirled and churned inside me, making me feel queasy.

Fortunately Mom was out with Uncle Luke and I had the house to myself. I threw myself onto my bed and cried like my heart was breaking. I cried because Koji learned the truth. I cried because I'd lied. I cried because I'd deceived Mrs. Yamada. She was the first adult to ever take me seriously about cooking. She treated me with respect, but I hadn't returned it. Not really.

I sobbed until my pillow was soaked in snot and tears. Flipping over onto my back, I threw my disgusting pillow onto the floor and scrubbed my face hard, as if that would wash away the shame.

There was only one person I wanted to talk to about this, only one person who would truly understand how I felt. But that also meant facing the fact that I'd also lied to my best friend.

Ugh! Everyone I loved was going to be super disappointed in me. I hoped that I could still keep what I'd done from my parents, but I knew now that I had to tell Charli. I needed her support, her advice, but most of all, I needed to be truthful and come clean with her. If Koji's reaction had been bad, Charli's would be exponentially worse if she found out from anyone but me.

I texted Charli and two seconds later she FaceTimed me. When I picked up, she went from happy to concerned in a flash.

"Sana!" she gasped. "What's wrong? What happened?"

I quirked my lips. "I look that bad, huh?"

It was great to see Charli's face. It had only been a few weeks since she'd left, but it felt like forever. I missed her. I needed her. My eyes began to well up again. Darn. I thought I'd already cried out all my tears.

"Sana," Charli said, worry tingeing her voice. "What's going on? You're scaring me."

I didn't even know where to start. The video? Cooking with Mrs. Yamada? No. I had to start with the one thing that had made me keep everything from her in the first place.

I took a big breath and dove in. "I've been hanging out with Koji Yamada."

She went from sympathetic to angry in the blink of an eye. "What did he do to you?" Her reaction surprised me. I'd thought she'd be mad at me, not Koji.

That made me cry fresh tears. Charli was upset, but it was all about protecting me and not at all about the secret I'd been keeping. That's the kind of best friend she was.

"Charli, it's not like that." I'd been the one who lied. There really was no good excuse for it. Then again, Koji hadn't even given me a chance to explain. All this back-and-forth was hurting my head.

She nodded. "Okay. I'm listening."

"I didn't tell you about it because when I tried, you were against me getting to know him."

She raised her eyebrow at me.

"I'm not blaming you. It's not your fault. I should have been more honest with you."

I told her everything. About meeting his mom, cooking with her, lying to his family about who I was, lying to my family about where I was, Harley, and our cooking video.

Charli was quiet for a long time, which was unusual. Her face flitted from emotion to emotion, like she wasn't sure how to feel. I was not a patient person, but I gathered all my strength to sit and wait. I knew it was a lot to take in.

"Wow," Charli finally said. "I've only been away for a couple of weeks, but it feels like you've lived a lifetime already."

I shrugged. "You've been busy, too." I hadn't meant to make it sound pouty, but that's how it came out.

She nodded. "You were lonesome."

"Yes, but also that's not the only reason I started hanging out with Koji."

"I know. He's cute. I can't blame you."

Ugh. No. This wasn't going smoothly at all. "I just wanted to get to know him, Charli. And he's nice. Funny and kind."

She cocked her head at me. "But he bailed on you, Sana. He didn't even listen to your side of things."

"Can you blame him? He and his family hate my dad."

"But your dad didn't do anything wrong! It's not like he put signs in front of that other restaurant that said 'Don't eat here.'"

"I know!"

"And you've been hanging out with Harley Lambert? I thought she'd moved away."

"You know her? Apparently she comes back every summer to stay with her dad."

Charli nodded. "Koji and Harley were tight in elementary school. A lot of other kids teased them that they were a couple, even in fourth grade."

"They weren't though, right?"

"Of course not. We were kids!" Charli shrugged. "No, it was more they were BFFs, joined at the hip. They hung out *all* the time."

"Were you friends? With Harley?" I asked.

Charli's cheeks puffed up with air and then deflated when she blew out a breath. "No. But I'm not really sure why. We just didn't like each other. She hung out with Koji and I was friends with Daniel Morrissey."

"Who?" The name sounded familiar.

"The boy Koji punched."

"Oh, so why don't you know what happened between them?"

Charli made a face. "Okay, so maybe Daniel and I weren't exactly friends."

I waited. Charli's cheeks turned pink. "Charli?"

"Ugh. I had a crush on Daniel."

"Wait." Now I knew why the name sounded familiar. "Doesn't Daniel Morrissey go to our school? Isn't he kind of a bully?"

"Yeah, he isn't much different from elementary school. It was a very short-lived crush. It turned out he wasn't a nice person."

"So let me get this straight. Back then, you had a crush on the guy Koji punched. And that's why you don't like Koji?"

"Hmmm. Maybe?" Charli rubbed her eyes. "Oh geez, I guess I was just harboring an old grudge. But still! Koji punched someone. And he got expelled."

I shook my head. "No way, Charlotte Boyce Hirai! You do not get to fall back on that now." Frustration bubbled and fizzed in my chest. "All this time I was scared to tell you about Koji because some bully didn't like him? It didn't have anything to do with him being dangerous."

Charli raised one hand. "Okay, okay. Don't get mad at me, Sana. I'm sorry."

I dropped my head back against the wall behind my bed, hard. "What a mess. Not only have I lost Koji as a friend, but now I won't have my cooking lessons with his mom, not to mention the fun videos Koji and I were making."

Suddenly Charli bolted up. "Wait. *This Is How I Roll* is your show?"

"Yes?" I didn't know why I answered like it was a question.

"Do you realize how popular it is?"

"What do you mean? You've seen it?"

She shook her head. "No, not yet. But at least four different people in my program have mentioned it. I kept meaning to watch it. Kiran thought I'd like the artsy concept. That's *you*?!"

Suddenly I was staring at Charli's dorm room ceiling as she dropped her phone. I heard her scrabbling around. When she picked up the phone again, she was on her laptop. And while I could only see her face, I heard the opening music for our show. I couldn't believe I'd never see Koji again and we wouldn't be doing this show together anymore.

Charli's eyes were bright and she smiled as she watched my first episode. Once the end credits ran, she clicked off and returned her attention to her phone.

"Sana! That was amazing! I'm mad I never thought of doing something like this with you. I mean, I've been watching crafting videos forever!"

I didn't say anything. But then I didn't need to. "Oh, Sana,"

Charli sighed. "I've been totally selfish. All we do is what I want to do, watch the videos I want to watch, and do the projects I want to do. You never complain."

"I love hanging out with you and doing all those crafts with you. I probably wouldn't have figured out the kawaii sushi without all that."

"I know, but you love to cook."

"You don't."

"Yeah, but we should do things you like, too. Besides, this isn't cooking! It's almost like sculpture."

"Well, I won't be doing it anymore. And I won't be cooking with Mrs. Yamada."

"No, listen up, Sana," Charli said, using that voice I loved, the one that made me feel completely supported. "Koji isn't the boss of you. You go talk to Mrs. Yamada and you tell her the truth. Let her decide if she can forgive you. Don't let Koji decide your fate."

She was right. I'd made this mess. I needed to try to clean it up.

# 28

I was grateful that I'd promised Mom I'd help her with the house project on her days off. It kept me busy and stopped me from thinking about Koji and what I had to do on Wednesday. I had to admit, it was fun working with Mom. On Monday we picked out pretty gray-and-white tiles for the kitchen floor, and on Tuesday we started prepping the cabinets for painting. Dad wasn't thrilled that we had to empty them. Dishes, pots, pans, and bowls were piled all over the living room. But he said he was pleased with how I'd grouped everything so he could still find things. I couldn't wait to cook in our new updated kitchen. It made me smile even though my heart was heavy with what I was about to do.

On Wednesday, I biked to Mrs. Yamada's house faster than usual, probably because I was being fueled by pure anxiety.

Better to get this over with. If I had to wait one more day—even one more hour—before I confessed, I might implode from stress.

"Sana, as always, you're right on time," Mrs. Yamada said as she let me into the house. "I was just setting up. I have leftover chicken, so I thought we'd make oyakodon. And today it's just the two of us. Koji has to work later, but I'm sure you knew that already."

I had every intention of telling her the truth right then, right there. But hearing that Koji wouldn't be coming for lunch meant I didn't have to rush out of there before he caught me cooking with his mom. It meant I could stay. This was the last time I would get to cook with her, my last lesson. I would savor every moment, soak up all the knowledge she had to share, and then I would confess.

"Do you know what oyakodon is?" Mrs. Yamada asked as we stepped up to the counter.

I inhaled the starchy scent of freshly steamed rice and shook my head, wishing I'd get to learn all of her homestyle dishes.

"*Oya* means *adult* and *ko* means *child*," Mrs. Yamada said. "It's a rice bowl made with chicken and eggs."

I stayed quiet for the entire lesson, committing to memory

not only the recipe but my time with Mrs. Yamada. I wanted to remember everything, the layout of the kitchen, the scent of lemons and rosemary, and her soothing voice.

When we were done cooking, I scooped rice into big bowls. The delicious aroma of rice, chicken, and eggs made my mouth water. Lifting some with my chopsticks, I slid the food into my mouth, closed my eyes, and chewed. The flavors reminded me a little of chicken noodle soup, the kind Mom made when I had a cold. It was comforting.

"You're quiet today, Sana. Is everything okay?"

This was the perfect moment to say something. But instead of opening my mouth to speak, I took another bite of oyakodon.

"Food can be healing," Mrs. Yamada said, watching me. "It can warm the soul and give you courage to say the things you need."

Wow. That did not feel random at all. "Koji told you?"

She shook her head. "He hasn't said anything specific, but I noticed a change. For a while he couldn't stop talking about you and the show, but the last couple of days he's been holed up in his room. When he does come out to eat, he's silent. Like you've been today."

I put my chopsticks down and shifted in my chair.

"You don't have to tell me anything if you're not comfortable."

I looked around the kitchen one last time. I'd miss all of this.

"I've been lying to you," I said, finally looking Mrs. Yamada in the eyes. "I've been keeping things from Koji, and from you."

"Oh?"

My throat felt dry and crackly. I took a gulp of water and pressed on. "I wasn't entirely truthful about who I am. My last name is Mikami."

Mrs. Yamada's eyebrows shot up.

"I'm sorry," I said quickly before she could yell at me or kick me out. "I didn't want to tell you who I really was because I love cooking with you. I feel horrible about lying. When Koji found out, he was angry and told me I couldn't cook with you anymore. Which is probably fair for the trouble I've caused." I spoke faster and faster and my voice went higher and higher.

"Slow down, Sana." She put a cool hand on my arm.

I gulped air. "I'm sorry," I said again, hoping I wouldn't start crying. That would totally make it worse. I was embarrassed enough.

"The thing I don't understand is, why would you lie about who you are?"

"I didn't want you to refuse to teach me how to cook."

She crinkled her forehead. "Why would I do that?"

"Koji told me that you hate my dad. That you all hate my dad." My voice cracked.

"I don't hate your dad, Sana. I don't even know him!"

Maybe she hadn't made the connection. "My dad is Chef Hiro, of Mikami Sushi."

"Yes, I know. But why would I hate him?"

"Because he made you lose your job?" I was confused.

"My job at the sushi restaurant?" When I nodded, she said, "Your dad had nothing to do with that."

"Koji said my dad's restaurant put the one you worked at out of business." I pondered. "But I know that my dad wouldn't have done that. I mean, not on purpose anyway."

"You're right," Mrs. Yamada said. "He didn't have anything to do with it. The owners of the restaurant wanted to move to the East Coast, where the rest of their extended family lived. They had already decided to close their business when your dad started working on opening his. It actually made them feel better knowing there would be a sushi place here after they left."

"But then why did Koji say—"

"I didn't tell the kids any details when I lost my job. I guess I should have. I didn't realize they would make such a big assumption. I'm sorry."

"You don't need to apologize to me," I said.

"I will talk to Koji and Yuri when they get home."

Mrs. Yamada and I finished eating our lunch in silence as my mind churned. She wasn't mad at me! Koji had been wrong about my dad. But he wasn't wrong about me lying to him. I wasn't sure how I would fix that, but my conversation with Mrs. Yamada gave me hope.

"Why didn't you apply to work at my dad's restaurant?"

"I did look into it, but the only job he'd advertised was for a hostess. My heart is in the kitchen and that's where I want to be."

"You are an awesome cook," I said. "I've been eating my dad's food all my life and I'm not lying when I say I think yours is just as good."

She smiled. "Thank you, Sana. That means a lot. I am thinking of going to culinary school."

"Nice." I didn't think she needed it. But maybe that would help her get a job in a restaurant? I wondered if I could talk to dad about hiring her. Although how would I explain how I knew her and her cooking?

As if Mrs. Yamada could read my thoughts, she suddenly exclaimed, "Sana! Does this mean your parents don't know where you've been all this time? While cooking with me? Recording with Koji?"

I guess I wasn't totally in the clear after all.

# 29

I'd been able to convince Mrs. Yamada to wait to talk to my parents. I wanted a chance to tell them everything first. She said she'd give me till the morning, so that meant I had to confess tonight. Dad wouldn't be home till eleven at least. I'd have a long wait ahead of me.

They were going to be really upset with me, but Mrs. Yamada agreed to keep giving me cooking lessons as long as she got to meet my parents and get their permission. I didn't blame her for not trusting me to do the right thing.

As much as I wanted to blame my lies on Charli for not being okay with me hanging out with Koji, or Dad for being so strict I worried he'd forbid me from cooking with anyone else, this was all on me. I'd made all the bad choices that led me here. There was never a good reason to lie.

At least I would have the next eight hours or more to

strategize. Maybe Charli could help me. I'd text her after dinner.

But my eight hours turned into eight seconds when I got home. Dad was already there, in our kitchen.

"What are you doing home?" I blurted out. "Why aren't you at the restaurant?"

He turned from the refrigerator and placed a bunch of carrots on the apricot-tiled counter. I couldn't wait till we put in the new one.

Dad smiled. "It does feel a little strange to be standing in my own kitchen so close to dinnertime. Ethan did a great job while I was busy with filming. I'm giving him the kitchen today."

"You are?!" Dad never let anyone be in charge of his kitchen.

"He's earned it. I'll be his sous-chef." Dad saw the look on my face and laughed. My heart filled with love. I'd missed him.

"You're cooking dinner for us?" I washed my hands in the kitchen sink.

"My seafood supplier delivered some amazing sablefish this morning. I marinated it in miso and I'm firing up the grill in the backyard." Dad nodded at the counter. "I also got some crab legs for a kani salad. Do you want to help?"

I was so surprised that I dropped the towel I'd been using to dry my hands. I quickly picked it up and replaced it with a clean towel, then grabbed an apron.

Dad pointed to the food on the counter. "What do we do first?"

My heart pounded with excitement. "Wash the vegetables." I scooped up cucumbers and carrots. As I washed them, Dad put a pot of water on the stove to boil.

Then I shucked corn. It was one of my least favorite things to do, but today it felt like I'd won a grand prize. Once he'd put the corn into the boiling water, he handed me a knife. "Slice the cucumbers. Thin, but not too thin."

Dad had taught me his thinness preference for cucumbers when I was ten. And though it had been over two years, I hadn't forgotten. While we worked side by side, he gave me instructions every few minutes. The aroma of rice steaming in the rice cooker made my stomach rumble.

"Well, this is a welcome sight." Mom walked in the door and slipped off her shoes. "I'm hungry!"

She gave Dad a quick kiss and then gazed at the counter full of ingredients.

"We just need to finish the salad and I'll get the fish on the grill," he told her.

"Great! I'll go change and wash up." Mom smiled at me fondly, knowing I was loving this.

I watched as Dad mixed his special ponzu-mayo dressing. "Is this recipe a secret?" I asked.

"I do have secret sauces, but this one isn't mine. I learned to make it when I was an apprentice in Japan. It's one of my favorites."

Excellent! I'd show this to Mrs. Yamada. Then I remembered that first I needed to confess to my parents and get permission if I wanted to keep cooking with her.

I set the table while Dad grilled the fish, considering my options. During dinner was probably best. Dad would nod at me while distractedly appreciating the taste of the meal. Mom would be too busy scooping crab salad into her mouth to comment. The scrumptious dinner would keep them both in decent moods. Maybe they wouldn't even get mad at me.

Wow. Was I ever wrong.

I waited until Mom had almost finished eating her crab

salad and Dad had taken his first bite of the miso-marinated fish, and then I leapt in, trying to go for a casual tone. "So, I've been meaning to tell you I've been taking cooking lessons. Mrs. Yamada is teaching me how to make Japanese dishes, like tamago. I've learned a lot and can't wait to cook for you both."

Mom and Dad both stopped eating and looked at me as if I'd stuck my chopsticks straight up into my rice bowl.

"What did you just say?" Mom asked.

"Um, I'm cooking?"

"But who is this person, this Mrs. Yamada?" Dad asked. He hardly ever raised his voice, but his low, quiet voice was unsettling.

I explained how I'd met her.

"You've been doing this since the start of summer? When? And why didn't we know about this?" Mom's voice got louder with each question.

"Because!" I shouted. My dad's eyebrows flew up, so I lowered my voice. "Because all I want is to learn how to cook and Dad refuses to teach me. Mrs. Yamada is happy to give me lessons!"

I looked at Dad, hoping he'd tell me I was wrong. That he'd

rather be the one to teach me. Or at least that if he didn't want to teach me, then I could learn from someone else. My stomach clenched as Dad stood up, folded his napkin, and said very quietly, "Go to your room, Susannah. Now."

Really? Like I was a child? I tossed my napkin onto the table and was about to stalk away, when Mom stopped me.

"Sana, wait."

I turned to face her, a smile ready on my face. Mom would defend me to Dad. She would understand passion, especially now that she'd found the same thing in renovating our house.

"Give us Mrs. Yamada's phone number," Mom said.

Right. As always Mom and Dad were a united front. Neither of them cared about what I thought or how I felt!

I jammed my finger hard against my screen to share the number to Mom's phone and stormed up the stairs to my room. And then felt angrier when I couldn't even slam my door because I didn't have a door to slam. I couldn't remember the last time I'd been sent to my room.

Scratch that. I did remember.

It was before we moved. In typical Mom and Dad fashion, they never explained anything to me. They'd dropped the news that they were selling our home and we were moving to Piper Bay without any warning. For weeks I'd worried that something horrible had happened—that Mom had gotten fired or Uncle Luke was sick or we were broke—and that was why we had to sell the house and move.

I'd been so distracted that I'd forgotten to study for a math test and got my first-ever C. Dad had lectured me on the importance of a good education. When I'd tried to change the subject and ask about the move, he'd just told me to worry about my grades and not about things that didn't concern me. Like moving to a whole new city didn't affect me. And later, when we were packing up the house—after Dad had already moved to Piper Bay—I'd tried to ask Mom why he'd left his job. Without answering me, she'd tried to distract me with how wonderful it would be to live near Uncle Luke and Charli. When I kept pressing, she'd sent me to my room.

Charli was the one who'd told me the details: Dad was following his dream of opening his own sushi restaurant.

So why should they be surprised that I didn't tell them anything? I'd learned it from them.

Now, just like when I was little, I had to eavesdrop to try to figure out what my parents were thinking. And since my room was a straight shot from the kitchen, I could hear as if I were still sitting at the table.

"I don't understand," Mom said. "I thought we could trust her."

"Maybe we need to hire a babysitter," Dad said.

Ugh. No! I was almost thirteen!

"Or a tutor," Mom said. "She could be studying this summer."

I *was* studying! Studying cooking! This was so unfair. I should be allowed to be a part of the conversation. I should be allowed to explain. I heard Mom get up. My heart pounded, thinking she was going to ask me to come downstairs. But instead she walked past the stairs to her room and closed the door. As Dad cleared the table, I sat at the top of the stairs, trying to keep myself from bursting downstairs to defend myself.

Dad had just started washing the dishes when Mom came back into the kitchen. I leaned down to listen.

"Well, I got ahold of Mrs. Yamada. She can come over tomorrow morning since she has the day off," Mom said.

My heart sunk. Mom would have to go into work late. I supposed the good news was that Dad wouldn't be there to meet

Mrs. Yamada. He wouldn't miss going into work for anything.

I tapped out a text to Charli and caught her up. At least my parents hadn't thought to take away my phone. Yet. Charli didn't respond. She was probably busy with her program. At least she was getting to practice art. Her dad supported her. My parents thwarted me at every turn. And now I was probably going to lose my cooking lessons with Mrs. Yamada.

# 30

By the next morning, Charli still hadn't texted me back and neither of my parents had come up to talk to me, not even to scold me or dish out punishment. Were they so angry they couldn't even look at me? I needed to know if I would still get to cook with Mrs. Yamada. I knew my video recordings with Koji were over for sure, but I didn't want to lose my lessons, too.

I could hear Mom and Dad in the kitchen talking, and from the aroma, cooking. Why was Dad still home? Even though I hadn't eaten a full dinner, I wasn't hungry. Regret sat heavy in my stomach. I'd stayed in bed later than normal, mulling over all the different scenarios that could play out. I knew it couldn't be good if Dad wasn't going into the restaurant this morning.

Plates clinked onto the kitchen table as Mom and Dad spoke in low tones. Then Mom climbed the stairs to my room, carrying a plate.

"Want something to eat?" she asked in a soft voice.

I sat up in bed, tugging on my hair. "Are you and Dad still mad at me?"

Mom placed a plate of grilled fish and rice onto my desk. "I think we're more disappointed than angry."

For some reason that felt worse.

When the doorbell rang, Mom nodded to me. "I expect you to stay in your room. We'll talk later."

"But I should at least introduce you to Mrs. Yamada," I said, even though I was still in my pajamas and had bedhead.

"You should have thought of doing that at the start of summer."

Hearing those words in that tone of disappointment, something I hadn't heard from Mom in many years, made me deflate with shame. Mom disappeared back down the stairs and I heard the front door creak open.

"Hello, Mrs. Yamada, please come in," Mom said. "I'm Lucy Mikami."

"Thank you. It's good to meet you. Please call me Andrea."

I heard Mrs. Yamada remove her shoes and follow my mom

into the kitchen. Well, if I couldn't be with them, I could at least hear everything they said.

"This is my husband, Hiro," Mom said.

"Welcome," Dad said. "Please sit."

Chairs scraped against the floor.

"These are for you," Mrs. Yamada said.

"Oh, they're beautiful."

I was dying to know what Mrs. Yamada had brought.

"My son grew them in our garden," she said.

"The rosemary smells amazing," Mom said. "Nihongoga hanase masuka?"

"Hai! Mochiron."

Oh great, they were going to speak Japanese. I might have been able to catch a phrase or word or two, but at the speed they were talking, it would be impossible to understand much.

I sighed, rolled over to face the wall, and, pulling the sheets to my chin, checked my phone. Nothing at all from Charli. You'd think she would have read my desperate texts by now. How late did she get in last night? I sent her a new text and waited. I debated texting my other friends, but while I knew they'd be supportive, the good feeling they'd give me would be temporary. What I needed was to fix this.

I went online and checked our *This Is How I Roll* channel. When I saw that the view counters continued to go up for the two episodes and the teaser clip, I sighed. What was going to happen now? I watched the videos over and over, trying to recapture the joy of making them and keep myself from telling stories about what was happening downstairs.

That's when it hit me. For as long as I could remember, my parents had kept things from me. I'd had to fill in the blanks from clues they left (and yes, eavesdrop) to make sense of what was happening. I'd been telling stories to myself. Just like Charli had made up a story about Koji being a bad influence. Just like Koji had made up a story about why his mom lost her job. I wanted to stop making up stories, but to do that I needed to know the facts.

I should have asked the right questions. I should have pressed for the truth. I should have told Charli and Mom and Dad what I wanted. Deep down, I believed they would forgive me. Eventually. They knew that lying wasn't my typical style.

But Koji and Mrs. Yamada did not. They hadn't known me

long, and what they did know was not a good look. They thought I was a liar, untrustworthy, and selfish—a person who snuck around behind people's backs. A wave of shame washed over me. No wonder Koji hated me. Did Mrs. Yamada hate me, too?

What was I going to do?

# 31

"Sana? Wake up, honey. We need to talk."

I opened my eyes to see Mom's face looming over me.

"Did Mrs. Yamada leave?" My voice was froggy as I sat up and rubbed my eyes.

"Just now." Mom settled on the bed next to me.

I glanced at the time. "Wow. You talked for a long time."

Mom smiled. A good sign. "We had a lot in common."

"So, how much trouble am I in?" I wanted to get this over with.

Mom blew out a breath, making her bangs flutter. "What I most want to know, Sana, is why. Why did you keep this a secret? Why did you feel you couldn't talk to us? Mrs. Yamada is perfectly nice. Sneaking around is not very smart at all. You need to let me know where you are and with whom for your safety. Why would you do something like that?"

I didn't even know where to start.

"Is it because of the boy? Her son?"

I shook my head. I mean, sure, I'd lied about what I was doing partly because of Koji, but it was so much more complicated. "I really wanted to learn how to cook. Mrs. Yamada seemed to want to teach me."

"If you had properly introduced us and asked for permission, we would have been fine with it."

"Maybe you would have," I said in a low voice. "But not Dad."

"What do you mean?"

I peered around Mom. "Where is he anyway?"

"The restaurant. Your dad's still letting Ethan run the show this week, but he's helping with prep."

When Mom got upset or needed to think, she went for a run. When Dad felt that way, he spent time in the kitchen. Then again, he did that all the time anyway.

"Oh." I wrapped my arms around my knees.

"Sana, what did you mean about Dad not being okay with you taking lessons from Mrs. Yamada?"

"Just that he doesn't want me to cook."

"That's not true."

I shrugged.

Mom cleared her throat. "What about your new friend? Harley? Did you make her up?"

I sighed. "No, but she's not my friend. She's Koji's."

"Okay." Mom closed her eyes for a long moment. When she opened them, she said, "Tell me about Mrs. Yamada's son."

I'd wanted to fix this. I'd wanted to talk. So I did. I told her how I met him. And what Charli's opinion of him was and how all the secrets and lies started. Which reminded me that I never did find out the story behind why Koji had been expelled. I'd been so worried about his questions for me that I hadn't pushed. Keeping secrets made it hard to ask others to be honest and forthcoming.

"He isn't a bad person, Mom. If he were mean or rude or even a bad influence, I wouldn't have hung out with him. He took me to meet his mom, like, immediately."

Mom shook her head. "You're too young to make these decisions all on your own. It's not that I don't trust your judgment, Sana. But you're still my daughter, my child. I need to know where you are and what you're doing so I can keep you safe."

Mom stood up and started pacing. "We've been too lenient.

I'm not blaming you, Sana, I'm blaming us. It's our job as your parents to, well, parent you. Things need to change."

My heart rattled in my chest. Not more change.

"I'm going to give notice at the hotel. I'm not quitting because of you. Dad's restaurant is doing well enough that we can afford it, and I want to work on the house. I really love renovating and decorating. Uncle Luke said maybe he can start hiring me out to do simple fix-ups for the houses he has on the market. And this way, you and I can spend more time together." Mom sat back down on my bed. "Sana, I worry about what could have happened. If things had gone wrong, if Koji and Mrs. Yamada hadn't been good people . . ." She gripped my leg, tightly. "That terrifies me."

"Oh. Mom. I'm sorry. I didn't think about that." I never intended to worry or upset my parents. I just hadn't wanted to deal with confrontation. "It's just . . . maybe I learned from you and Dad not to talk about things."

"What are you saying?"

"You never discuss anything with me." I raised a hand to stop Mom from interrupting, because if she did, I might never find the courage to say how I felt. "I get that maybe when I was a little kid, you didn't need to explain things to me. But by the time I was ten, I really wanted to know what was going on. You only talked to each other, after I went to bed. And I know it was wrong to try to listen in, but it was the only way I could find out anything."

"I don't understand," Mom said. "What things?"

"Everything! All of a sudden I was at Alana's every day after school until you got off work. I mean, I loved hanging out with her, but you didn't discuss it with me. And I had to listen in to find out you'd signed me up for swimming lessons because Dad never learned and wanted to make sure I knew how. I wanted to be part of the conversation!" I swallowed my frustration. "But especially when you decided to move here. When I asked why we had to leave San Francisco, you told me not to worry about it. But I did. I worried and made up stories about why we might be moving, and none of them were good. I had to find out the truth from Charli."

Mom sighed. "We didn't want to burden you. Like I said, as your parents we want to protect you. And there are things adults have to deal with that you don't yet. Dad and I just want you to enjoy your life and be carefree."

"But don't you see? How can I be carefree when I'm wondering what's really going on?"

"Sweetie, I didn't realize you felt this way." Mom patted my leg. "I'm not trying to make excuses, but you must know by now that Dad has a hard time expressing his feelings and thoughts. He's not comfortable talking about what's going on mostly because of the way he was brought up. It was something I had to adjust to when we were dating and in the early years of our marriage. I know he loves me—loves *us*—by his actions.

"But I can see how you might misinterpret his silence or the few words he does say because he offers them without much explanation. While the burden shouldn't be on you, it might help if you ask more pointed questions to try and get Dad to explain what he's thinking or feeling."

I got what Mom was saying, and I knew Dad wasn't the overly affectionate type. I really did know that he loved me, but I didn't know how he felt about my love for cooking.

Mom put her arm around me. "Maybe we can all try, as a family, to be better at talking about what's going on and sharing our feelings."

That would definitely be a move in the right direction.

"But that doesn't mean you're off the hook," Mom warned. "Your dad and I still need to discuss your punishment."

A lump the size of an onigiri formed in my throat. "I have one more thing to tell you."

Mom's eyes widened. "There's more?"

I got up from my bed and retrieved my laptop. Making sure Mom could see the screen, I loaded the first episode of *This Is How I Roll* and hit play. I was too nervous to watch her reaction, so I focused on the video. Even if it got me in more trouble, I felt proud of what I'd created.

When it was over, I said, "There's another episode and a teaser clip, too. And we recorded a third episode, but it never got uploaded."

Mom closed my computer and placed it on my desk. When she turned to look at me, her face was unreadable.

"I feel like I don't know you anymore," she said. "You're not going anywhere tomorrow."

Mom left my room, her back a little rounded as she descended the stairs. I had no idea what to expect tomorrow, but it wouldn't be good.

# 32

The next morning I paced my room, wondering when Mom and Dad would talk to me about everything. Waiting was the worst! Fortunately my phone started to ping with a slew of messages. A welcome distraction.

**Charli:**
OMG I'm so sorry I missed your texts! I'd left my phone at my raku pottery lesson & had to wait till last night to get it.
How are you? I talked to Dad & he caught me up on everything. I'm sorry you got busted. I hope you're okay. Dad said Mrs. Y talked to your parents?
I know you're probably sleeping so call me when you get this! Well, after my classes today. I miss you!

**Esme:**
Hello? Why no more eps?

**Liv:**
Also, why have you gone silent?

**Alana:**
Maybe she's too big of a star to talk w us anymore. 😊

**Liv:**
Seriously S why aren't you answering?

**Esme:**
She's sleeping.

**Liv:**
Maybe now, but not for like the last week!

**Alana:**
We miss you Chef Sana! I hope you're okay.

**Esme:**
Also, we want to hear more about Koji!

Tears pooled in my eyes. I missed them, too. But I just didn't know what to say. Everything felt so up in the air.

Suddenly I heard a racket from the kitchen. I knew those sounds well. The kiss of the fridge door opening. The soft thump of items being laid out on the counter. The clink of a pan set on the stove top. I tucked my phone into my pajama pocket and headed downstairs.

"Dad?" Having him around so often this week was unsettling, even if it was nice. "Why are you home?"

Dad continued organizing ingredients at the counter. He wouldn't meet my eyes. "Ethan's running dinner service again."

It was Friday. The Chef's Choice meal. "He's doing omakase?" My voice went up an octave.

"Yup."

I didn't know what to say. That was . . . incredible. I was really happy for Ethan.

"I'm going back later to help out, but in the meantime, come here."

I scooted into the kitchen. There was no way I'd test Dad's patience by being slow to respond, even if I was a little nervous about what he was going to say to me.

"Mrs. Yamada said she taught you how to make several dishes." Dad stepped back. "And Mom showed me your videos. Kawaii sushi. Nice concept and good execution."

I was stunned. Praise was definitely not what I'd been expecting from my dad.

He nodded at the counter as he perched on a stool, like a teacher. Or a judge. "Go ahead and make tamago."

"Now?" My voice squeaked.

"Mochiron." Of course.

I washed my hands and put on my apron. Despite the nervous rumblings in my stomach, I squared my shoulders, hoping to give off an air of confidence I didn't quite feel. All the ingredients I needed had been set out for me. I took a deep breath and started by making dashi. As I chopped and measured and stirred, everything around me faded away. It was me and the ingredients—nothing else mattered. Not Dad's judgment, not Koji's hatred, not my worries. I focused only on making tamago, on how cooking a dish for someone you cared about showed them how you really felt. By the time I slid the perfectly rolled tamago onto a plate, I was positively radiant. I felt like beams of light must have been shining from my body.

My smile wavered slightly as I set the plate on the counter in front of my dad. Then my nerves disappeared because Dad was . . . smiling. Like full-on grinning in a way I hadn't seen in years.

"Dad?"

"Susannah! Sugoi!" Dad started rattling on in Japanese, but even if I couldn't understand what he was saying, I recognized the enthusiasm in his voice. He took a knife and sliced the tamago into eight even pieces, then lifted the plate and scrutinized the tamago, his eyes bright. Popping a piece into his mouth, he chewed slowly. This was the real test. I could hardly breathe as I waited for his verdict. Dad didn't say a word as he grabbed a spoon, dipped it into my dashi, and tasted it. I was sure it had taken a ton of willpower for him to stay seated and quiet the whole time I was cooking. While he contemplated my final product, impatience and anxiety swirled inside me. So I used that nervous energy to clean up.

As I washed dishes, Dad came over and popped a piece of the tamago into my mouth. I chewed, swallowed, and smiled. It was my best one yet.

Instead of only worrying about Dad's opinion, I focused on the warm water flowing over my hands, the feel of the soapy sponge sliding across the pan, the sound of the fridge opening and closing. Being in the kitchen always made me happy, but being in the kitchen with Dad brought me the most joy. I wished he understood that.

I placed the pan into the drainer and Dad quickly snagged it. Had I not washed it well enough? When I turned to look at him, he was drying the pan. Was he annoyed I hadn't dried it right away?

"Susannah, if you're done, come here."

He didn't sound annoyed or upset.

"I'm going to teach you how to make atsuyaki tamago. It's thicker, with no layers. But it takes time. A lot more time."

I slumped. My tamago was a failure. I should have known better. Dad totally looked down on homestyle cooking.

"What's wrong?" he asked as I blinked back tears. When I didn't answer, his forehead wrinkled with concern. "Susannah—"

"You hated my tamago!" I cried.

"What? No!" Dad put his hands on my shoulders and turned me to him. "It was perfect!"

"Really?" He rarely ever used that word to describe food.

Definitely not anything I'd made. "You're not just saying that to make me feel better?"

He raised his eyebrows with a tilt of his head. "Have you ever known me to say something just to make anyone feel better?"

I quirked my lips. "No. But why didn't you say anything when you tasted my food?"

Dad sighed and dropped his hands. "Mom said you told her we don't talk to you enough about what we're thinking or feeling. I suppose you're right. I grew up with parents who only talked to me to tell me when I was disappointing them. Which was often. As soon as I turned eighteen, I left for Japan just to get far away. While I was there, I didn't really have any close friends, just colleagues, and we didn't have deep conversations. That is not an excuse. It's just me, explaining to you that expressing myself doesn't come naturally."

"Oh." But really how was I to know all that when he'd never shared his story with me?

"Give us time, Susannah. We'll do better. We can all learn how to change and improve at what we do, including parenting." Dad waved to the counter. "Would you like to learn how to make tamago my way?"

"It's not because you think Mrs. Yamada's homestyle cooking isn't as good as high end?"

Now Dad looked exasperated. "Of course not! Where is all this coming from? When have I ever looked down on any style of cooking?"

"You never cook all of Mom's favorites. You stopped teaching me how to cook. Your restaurant is fine-dining sushi. And I overheard you telling Mom about how your boss wouldn't hire a woman to be a sushi chef. So maybe you don't think I should be a chef either. Maybe that's why you stopped cooking with me!"

Dad looked at me for a long beat and then my heart sunk as he took off his apron and folded it, placing it onto the stool. Now I'd lost my chance to learn how to make his tamago.

"Come with me," Dad said, walking out of the kitchen.

# 33

I followed Dad into my parents' bedroom. He pulled out Mom's desk chair for me. When I sat, Dad opened her laptop and moved the cursor to a folder labeled "The Mikami Way." That was the working title of Baxton's documentary. Had they finished editing the film already? It didn't seem possible.

"Baxton sent me a few files as a preview," Dad explained.

He double-clicked to expand the folder and scrolled, stopping at a file called "Interview 5." Dad opened it and a video started to play.

The screen showed Dad and Baxton seated next to each other at the sushi bar at Mikami Sushi. It was odd to see Dad on the customer side of the bar. The camera zoomed to a close-up of him.

"It seems like your daughter takes after you, at least in her passion for cooking," Baxton said. "How do you feel about that?"

I tensed, but even as I was afraid of Dad's answer, I couldn't help but lean forward to listen.

Onscreen, Dad shifted in his chair as he removed his sushi chef's cap. The camera focused in on his hands as they twisted the white cap, then zoomed out to a shot of Dad again. His face looked contemplative. And torn.

"I'm proud," Dad said in a quiet voice. His words made my heart stutter with hope. "But I also worry."

"What do you mean?" Baxton asked.

"I had a challenging childhood," Dad said. "My parents both immigrated from Japan and wanted me to be a success. To them that meant exceptional scholastic achievement and a career in medicine. But I struggled in school and my grades were not the kind that would get me into the type of college they wanted. I was a disappointment and they never stopped telling me so.

"On top of that, my parents had an unhappy marriage. I just wanted to get away. I had no idea what I wanted to do. I hadn't been allowed to have hobbies or play sports. I was very much a loner. I'm bilingual because my parents spoke Japanese at home, so I saved every penny I could and as soon as I graduated, I took off for Tokyo.

"When I got there, I stayed in a hostel and took whatever job I could get. I worked for a short time as an English tutor, but like I said, school wasn't really my thing, not as a student and certainly not as a teacher. One of the other instructors got me a job as a dishwasher at an American chain restaurant in the Roppongi district and I worked my way up. I found a sense of peace when I was chopping and stirring."

I nodded. I felt the same.

"After a year of working as a line cook, I grew bored. At times I worried that perhaps I'd been wrong—that cooking wasn't my passion after all. But then I noticed that it was the dishes that bored me, not the cooking. I quit and found a job in a sushi restaurant that served cuisine that spoke to me deeply. I had to start at the bottom again—washing dishes, working long shifts—but I was fascinated by everything that went on in that kitchen. The chef took notice and after a year of hard work and proving my commitment, he took me on as his apprentice. I was very lucky."

All this was brand-new to me. I'd never heard Dad's story.

"It was when I became Iida-san's apprentice that I knew deep in my heart that this was what I was meant to do, who I was meant to be. But it was hard work with long hours. I prepped, cooked, cleaned, and cleaned some more. It took years before I was allowed to make sushi."

"This was your joy, your passion." Baxton's voice startled me; I'd been so lost in Dad's story.

Dad nodded, looking solemn. "I am very grateful. But for this reason I want my daughter to enjoy her childhood. To dabble and discover, to play and grow and learn. It makes me happy to see Susannah try new and different things."

Suddenly an image popped into my head, a memory I hadn't thought about in years: Dad taking me to a music store in San Francisco when I was little, and laughing as I tried different instruments. It didn't matter if it was bongo drums or an accordion, he'd let me play and experiment. And when in the end I didn't feel compelled to learn to play any instrument, he'd let it go. No pressure.

Warmth like fresh-baked bread spread in my chest as I shook the memory away and returned my focus to the interview clip.

"I took great pleasure in teaching my daughter how to cook when she was young. It amazed and impressed me to see her take to it so naturally. And it was fun. In fact, for a while it was one of the very few things I enjoyed, because around that time, I was starting to struggle at my job."

"This was at the sushi restaurant in San Francisco?"

"Yes. Working there had begun to feel more and more like drudgery. And my boss and I often clashed."

"About what?"

"We were short-staffed with only two sushi chefs. I was overworked and needed help. An outstanding candidate applied, but my boss refused to consider her because she was a woman. He thought a woman couldn't be a good sushi chef. We had a huge argument and I quit."

I gasped. Dad had quit? Over this? I had no idea!

Baxton spoke again. "So let me bring you back to my original question. Your daughter seems to have a strong passion and talent for cooking, particularly Japanese cooking. Do you encourage her?"

Dad frowned. "I was conflicted. And still am. I'm proud of her, but I don't want her to decide now what she wants to do later. She should be having fun, not striving for perfection like I was when I was her age. Perfection isn't attainable. Plus restaurant life is difficult. Long hours standing on your feet, hard work, little time for anything else. Because I have an excellent and responsible staff, I have now started to think it's possible to spend a little more time at home with my family."

I felt another flutter of hope. Dad might be home more often! Maybe we could cook together after all. Or at least do things together as a family, like go hiking or to the movies.

Onscreen, Dad cleared his throat and continued, "But let me answer your question. I would very much like to encourage my daughter in the kitchen. I just also want her to explore other options, to see if other things bring her joy. I want her to have choices."

"And if she decides to follow in your footsteps?" Baxton asked.

I curled my fingers and pressed my fists against my legs.

Dad looked right at the camera, right at me. "I would do everything I can to help her on her journey."

The clip ended and I blinked at the screen. Then I swung around to face Dad.

"You aren't trying to keep me from cooking?" I asked.

"Of course not."

"Then why did you stop teaching me?"

Dad perched on the desk, facing me, and ran his hand through his hair. I waited out the seconds, the minutes, knowing he sometimes needed time before speaking.

"Do you remember the last time we cooked together in San Francisco?" Dad asked.

Of course I did. That moment was seared in my brain. "I messed up. I used sugar instead of flour in a roux for the curry. I hadn't been paying close attention." I frowned thinking about how that had been the thing that had proved to Dad that I was unworthy.

"Yes," he said quietly. "And I yelled at you."

I nodded.

"I made you cry." Dad's shoulders sagged. "And while I had never dared shed tears in front of my parents when they berated me, I knew exactly how you felt. I never wanted to be like my parents, and there I was repeating their mistakes, making you feel small."

"Dad! You yelled at me once. And I was the one who messed up." I'd heard Dad be sharp with his staff a few times. He was never cruel, but he didn't have patience for laziness or distracted behavior.

"The first time I held you after you were born, that first day in the hospital, I made a promise to you, Susannah. I promised to make you feel safe, to not place expectations on you, to make sure you had a happy childhood. When I made you cry that day, I knew I'd failed. You were ten—of course you're going to make a mistake or two!" Dad shook his head. "So that's why I stopped cooking with you. I didn't want to turn something you loved into something you feared. And I wanted you to be free to do other things."

"That's not fair, Dad," I said. "First, you never told me any of that! I have thicker skin than you think. Yeah, I cried, but that didn't mean I thought you didn't love me! I wanted to keep cooking with you. I kept asking you to, but you refused. *That* broke my heart. Not the one time you shouted at me."

Dad deflated. "The truth is I got busy scouting a location for my own restaurant, worrying about money, and preparing to move us to a brand-new place." He shook his head. "I'm sorry it seemed like I didn't want to teach you anymore. That wasn't true and still isn't. I was overwhelmed, but I should never let life get too hectic to spend time with you, Susannah. That will change,

I promise. If you want to cook—if it makes you happy—then of course I'll teach you."

The fuzzy feeling that buzzed in my chest grew warm with happiness and . . . hope. Then I remembered something.

"So you're not upset that Mrs. Yamada isn't teaching me high-end cooking?"

"Your mother and I are disappointed that you snuck around, but no, not that you're learning from her. She seems to be very talented. There aren't 'better' ways of cooking, Susannah. I hope you don't think that because I run a traditional omakase sushi restaurant that I look down upon other styles of cooking. You follow your heart. That's what's important. I didn't stop cooking Mom's favorite meals because of that. Like I said, I got busy. I was hardly cooking at home at all." Dad placed his hand on my shoulder. "I like that you're learning from Mrs. Yamada."

"Does this mean I can still cook with her?"

He smiled. "I hope that in between your lessons you will have time to learn from me again, too."

I flew out of the chair and flung myself at Dad, wrapping my arms around him. He hugged me back.

"Now, how about we make tamago?" Dad asked.

My stubborn and stoic dad was making an effort to change. For me. That's how I knew, no matter what, everything was going to be okay.

And that if I wanted anything else in my life to change, I would have to make it happen.

# 34

Because we'd come to an understanding, Mom and Dad decided not to ground me after all, and I was supremely grateful for that. I retained the use of my phone and laptop, and I was allowed to go to Mrs. Yamada's on Wednesdays to resume my cooking lessons. The new thing was that I had to be supervised at all times. Not that I was going to be chained to an adult, but I was no longer going to be allowed to go off on my own.

Honestly? While I didn't love the loss of freedom and trust my parents had in me, there were definitely silver linings. I continued to work with Mom on the kitchen renovation. And the best part? A few times a week, I got to be at Dad's restaurant during the day before the restaurant opened. I wasn't doing any prep or cooking, but I helped out by cleaning, washing dishes, and organizing. That was all I ever wanted, to spend time with Dad in his restaurant.

Plus it freed Manny up to do more prep. He didn't want a career at the restaurant or to take on more hours during his last year of coursework for his degree in microbiology. And he wasn't the only one with other aspirations. Dad had been giving Ethan more independence at the restaurant because Ethan would be striking out on his own come fall. I would miss him, but after over five years apprenticing under Dad, he was ready to try his hand at being a chef in his own right.

Dad would need a new sous-chef. I wanted it to be me, of course, but I knew that wouldn't happen. He told me he'd consider it after I graduated from college, which was forever away. So I suggested the perfect person to Dad and he actually listened to me.

When I walked into Mrs. Yamada's kitchen the following Wednesday, she wrapped me in a big hug. "Sana! I don't know how to thank you." She pulled back and smiled at me.

I tucked my chin. "I didn't do anything."

"You know that's not true. If you hadn't told me about the opening at your dad's restaurant and suggested me to your dad, I never would have gotten the job."

I followed her into the kitchen. "Well," I admitted, "maybe I helped a little, but you got it all on your own. One thing you should know about my dad is that he never says or does anything just to be kind. If he hired you, he must believe in you and your skills."

Mrs. Yamada nodded and smiled. "All the same, I am grateful. This is the kind of job I've dreamed about and now I won't have to spend money on going to culinary school. I'll be learning from the best in the field and getting paid for it!"

I blushed. I was truly happy for Mrs. Yamada. Dreams could come true. The fact that I was still getting to take lessons with her proved it.

But when I looked around the kitchen, I realized nothing was laid out on the counter. "We're not cooking today?"

"I think it's time you and Koji cleared things up. I made bento for the two of you to share." She nodded to two containers stacked on the kitchen table. "Make yourself comfortable. I'll be outside gardening and Yuri is in her room, so no one will bother you."

Before I had a chance to come up with an excuse, she was out the door. I stared at the clock. Koji still wasn't due back for another hour. Did Mrs. Yamada really expect me to just sit here and wait?

I could use the time to come up with a plan. Koji and I hadn't exchanged one text since he'd told me to stay away. I wondered if he thought about me even half as often as I thought of him. Probably not.

If only I'd been able to tell him the truth on my own, without Harley's meddling. But then I might never have come clean. All of us—me, Koji, Harley, Yuri, and Charli—had been telling ourselves stories about why difficult things happened to make ourselves feel better about them. This wasn't really Harley's fault.

I put on my shoes and found Mrs. Yamada in the front flower bed, weeding.

"I hope you're not leaving," she said, shading her eyes with her gloved hand.

"No. But since I have some time, can you tell me where Harley lives?"

A few minutes later, I was standing on her porch. I rang the doorbell three times before Harley came to the door. She definitely did not look happy to see me.

"What do you want?" she said without a trace of friendliness.

"To apologize."

Her mouth opened, but no words came out.

"At first I was mad at you for ratting me out to Koji, of course. But what I did was all on me. I was the one who didn't tell the truth about who I was. I'm not angry at you. Not that you care. Still, I'm sorry for lying to you."

Harley was quiet. I shrugged and turned to go back to Koji's. I'd done what I intended. I hadn't expected her to have the warm fuzzies for me. It was obvious she didn't like me. Even though Charli said my superpower was making friends, I knew that I'd blown it with Koji and Harley.

"Hey, wait!" She stepped out onto the porch. "Um, I'm sorry, too. I shouldn't have said anything to him."

I shrugged. "It's fair. I was the one who was lying."

"I could have talked to you about it first."

"Maybe. But we aren't exactly friends."

"True." Harley picked at an invisible thread on her pink paisley dress. "I wasn't very nice to you."

"Because Koji."

She sighed. "Because Koji."

"You like him."

Harley tilted her face up toward the trees like she was looking at something. "I had a big crush on him in fourth and fifth grade, before he moved. And then hung on to it while he was away. But I don't know. We were kids then. And he obviously only thinks of me as a friend."

"Friendship can grow into more." As Alana always said.

Harley shook her head. "No, not this one. He told me last week."

"He said that?" I was surprised. It didn't seem like a very nice thing to do.

"He only likes me as a friend. His best friend." She smiled and shrugged. "At least now I know."

We stood there in the warm sun. I wasn't sure what to say. That must have taken a lot of courage on Koji's part to speak a truth that might hurt someone he cared about.

"He likes you," she said. There was no anger there. And her words made my heart flutter.

"Maybe he might have before, but not anymore." The best I could hope for was try to be friends with him again.

"I lied, too." Harley said, now staring at her pink painted toenails.

"What do you mean?"

"When I said that Koji was a flirt and got tired of girls easily. I made that up. That's not true at all. Koji is a really nice guy."

"Oh."

"I thought by getting rid of you, I'd have a chance with him. But ever since you stopped coming around, he's been really down. When I go to his house, he just sits on the couch while we watch TV and I do all the talking. He obviously misses you. Just saying."

Harley stepped into her house, and gently, quietly, shut the door.

# 35

I was at the Yamadas' kitchen sink drying my hands when I heard Koji's voice coming through the door.

"Thanks, Mom! Bento sounds great!"

I froze, rooted in place. His head tipped down as he slipped off his shoes, and my heart swooshed in loops in my chest and landed with a bounce in my stomach. He looked amazing in his Earth-Love Landscaping shirt, streaked with soil and grass stains, the sleeves rolled as usual. His skin glowed with sweat. I couldn't look away, and when he finally lifted his head, our eyes locked.

Neither of us moved for a few long seconds. Then I started fidgeting uncontrollably. I didn't know what to do with the sudden burst of nervous energy that shot through me.

Koji finally broke the silence. "What are you doing here?"

His voice wasn't mean or loud, but it wasn't the friendly tone I was used to.

I nodded to the table. "Your mom made us lunch. She thinks we should talk."

Without another word, he walked over to me and stopped. For a brief second I thought he meant to hug me and I moved toward him, but then he quickly sidestepped around me to use the sink. My face burned with embarrassment. I strode over to the kitchen table like that was what I'd intended.

Koji poured lemonade for both of us, and when he set my glass in front of me, I thanked him. Harley said Koji liked me and that he'd been sad. That thought gave me the courage to say the things I had to get off my chest. He'd been brave enough to tell Harley how he felt. I needed to be able to do the same with him.

Koji sat down, and I started to talk before he had the chance to say anything else. There was no way I would be able to eat until I apologized and had a chance to explain myself.

"I'm really sorry for lying about who I am. I don't have a good excuse because there is no good reason to lie, especially to a friend."

Koji straightened his chopsticks in front of him and said, "I get why you didn't want to say who your dad was after Yuri and I told you how much we hated him and his restaurant. Mom explained everything. I know it wasn't your dad's fault she lost her job." He took a deep breath and looked at me, and for a brief second I forgot how to breathe. "And I guess I should thank you. Mom is over-the-moon happy about her new job working for your dad this fall."

I nodded. "My dad's happy, too."

"So," Koji said, now twirling one of his chopsticks between his fingers like it was a pen. I was pretty sure Mrs. Yamada would scold him for playing with his utensils. "While I get why you would have kept who you are a secret from me, I don't get why you didn't want your parents knowing you were here or why you had to be anonymous on our videos. Why keep us a secret from your family?"

It was time for the full truth. "Charli didn't want me to hang out with you. So I kept it from her and couldn't tell my parents because if my mom told my uncle, he would tell Charli, and then she'd yell at me. Plus I wasn't sure my dad wanted me to learn how to cook. But I was wrong about that."

Koji frowned. Wow. Even when he frowned he was beautiful. "Why would she be mad if you and I are friends?"

"She thought you'd be a bad influence."

"What? Why?" And then realization dawned. "Oh, because I got expelled in fifth grade."

I nodded and shrugged at the same time.

"You never asked me about it."

"I kinda did," I said. "But yeah, I didn't try too hard because I was afraid you would ask me questions I didn't want to answer."

"Okay," he said. "Ask me now."

"Why did you get expelled in fifth grade?"

Koji replaced his chopstick back on the table. "I punched Daniel Morrissey."

I, of course, knew that much from Charli. "I hope there's more to that story," I said.

A brief flash of Koji's dimple continued to buoy my hopes that we would be okay. "He was a bully, but a stealthy one. Perfect teacher's pet, but if he didn't have an audience? Cruel and mean. He kept giving me a hard time about my parents' divorce. I was able to pretty much ignore him until he said my dad left because my mom was a loser. No one talks about my mom like that. So, I punched him."

"Ah." Not that I condoned violence, but it was sweet that fifth-grade Koji was just as protective of his mom then as he was now.

"The school had a zero-tolerance policy. Mom and my dad were disappointed. And you know the rest. I was sent to LA for sixth grade to live with my uncle. And it was good for me to get away after my parents split. I was really angry back then. When I moved back home last summer, Mom was worried I'd have a reputation." He laughed. "So my dad pays for me and Yuri to go to a private school."

I sighed. "If only I'd asked you in the beginning, we would have avoided all these misunderstandings. Either way, I should have never lied."

"Yeah, Yuri gave me a big ol' lecture about honesty."

"She did?"

"Yeah, well, she pointed out that it was obvious that Harley liked me as more than a friend and how rude it was for me to pretend not to know, while I was kind of starting to have feelings for another girl." Koji's cheeks turned pink.

My face warmed. "Oh." I didn't know what else to say.

"I talked to Harley and cleared things with her. She is my very best friend . . ."

I nodded. Pretty much what Harley had said.

"But she isn't you. I miss you, Sana," Koji said.

I gasped quietly, almost under my breath. "I miss you, too," I said quickly before I lost my nerve. The big lesson I'd learned so far this summer was to say what I meant to the people who mattered. "I miss doing our cooking show, I miss talking and laughing with you, I miss hearing you talk about gardening, I miss eating with you. But yeah, mostly, I just miss you."

Koji picked up his chopsticks and then put them down again. Slowly, he reached across the table and held my hand. His palm was warm, calloused. Familiar.

"So," he said. "I want to be clear. What I really want is that we can be . . . more than friends." He squeezed my hand.

My mind and my heart were doing somersaults. "What?"

This time his dimple appeared as he smiled full-on. "I like you, Sana."

Like. Not liked.

"It was a bad move to bail on you," he continued. "I want

to take you to the beach, but Mom tells me you're kind of on lockdown?"

I nodded.

"Got it. Is it okay to come by your house?"

My face felt like it was being seared over a burner with the flame on high. "That would be great."

Koji got up and walked around to my side of the table. He put his hand out, and when I took it, he pulled me to my feet.

"Can we start over, then? Get to know each other for real? Truths only."

I nodded. "Truths only."

Koji stepped closer until we were barely two inches apart. And even though my heart was pounding so hard it hurt, I didn't want to lie anymore, especially to myself. I tilted my chin up to him.

He smiled down at me. "This is okay?" he asked.

"It's okay," I said in a whisper.

As we both leaned forward and our lips met, I felt Koji smile against my mouth. My first kiss. It lasted less than a second and forever at the same time.

"Oh, good!" Yuri said loudly as she clomped into the kitchen. "I'm glad you made up. Koji's moping was getting on my nerves."

Koji and I stepped apart, smiling at each other.

Nothing could ruin this moment.

Our moment.

# Epilogue

I double-checked to make sure I had all the ingredients lined up in front of me on the counter. My hands were a little sweaty, so I wiped them on my brand-new apron. Glancing behind me, I made sure the sign Charli had made wasn't crooked. THIS IS HOW I ROLL WITH SANA MIKAMI. It had a nice ring to it! The font was Charli's own design and she'd painted a sushi roll in place of the *o*. Kawaii nigiri dotted the border. Charli had really outdone herself, and had gone the extra mile to mail it to me in time for filming.

"Everything looks good," Koji said from the opposite side of the counter.

I smiled at him. Over the last two weeks we'd spent almost every day together. On Mondays and Tuesdays when Mom was home, Koji came over after work and helped us with renovation stuff. Plus he'd been working on our yard. I spent Wednesdays taking lessons from Mrs. Yamada and hanging out with Koji. And today we were back to filming our show.

To say Koji and I had gotten very comfortable around each other was more than fair. Best of all, we had fun together.

"Are you ready, superstar chef?" Koji asked. "Let's start filming. Time is money!"

I smirked. Then wiped my palms on my apron again.

"Chef Hiro? Mom? Are you both ready?" Koji asked.

Dad and Mrs. Yamada materialized next to me. Dad gave me a reassuring smile and nodded.

"On one. Here we go. Five, four, three," Koji said, and then finished the count flashing two fingers and then pointed at me.

I smiled at the camera. "Hi! Welcome back to *This Is How I Roll*. You'll notice we have a whole new format. I'm Sana Mikami and today we're making kawaii sushi in a special location with special guests."

I waited a beat knowing the camera was panning back to a wider shot. "We're at Mikami Sushi today and our guests are Chef Hiro, who is the owner of this restaurant *and* my dad, and his soon-to-be sous-chef, Mrs. Yamada."

As I talked about the cat and dog omusubi I was going to

be creating and listed the ingredients, Dad and Mrs. Yamada took turns lifting the items to show to the camera. I started the demo, and the time flew. In what felt like two blinks, we were done filming.

"And cut!" Koji called.

I grinned, feeling on top of the world.

"That was great," Baxton said, stepping forward to the counter. He turned to the crew. Griff gave a thumbs-up and Harley mimicked him as she handed over the reflector shield she'd been holding.

"You're a star, Sana," she said, grinning. When I'd told her she could help film with Baxton's crew, she'd screamed so loud my ears rang for hours.

Shelby turned off the camera. "You're still One-Take Sana!"

I ducked my head in embarrassed pleasure.

"That's my girl," Dad said, placing a warm hand on my shoulder.

I'd prepared enough kawaii rice balls for everyone. Dad brought the rest out from the kitchen and passed them out at the bar.

"You were great," Koji said, standing very close to me. "I can't believe this is going to be in Baxton Ferguson's documentary!"

"Well, it's only going to be a short clip and shown after the credits."

"That's still awesome," Harley said.

Even more awesome was the fact that Baxton was going to send us a full edited version for us to upload onto our YouTube channel. We would have a Baxton Ferguson–produced piece!

"So, back to regular filming at my house next week?" Koji asked, holding my hand.

We smiled at each other.

"Yep!" Harley said.

She was actually pretty cool to be around. Charli would be returning soon, and Harley wasn't going back to Seattle for another two weeks. My cousin had promised she'd give both Koji and Harley a chance. Alana, Liv, and Esme were coming out to spend the weekend and they were thrilled to meet Koji.

As we sat down to eat, everyone oohed and aahed over my creations.

"It looks like there will be two generations of Mikami chefs at this restaurant," Baxton said.

I smiled at Dad.

"The world is your oyster," he told me.

"Mmm, I love oysters," Shelby said.

Now that I knew I had my parents' support, and that my friendships were solid, I truly felt like I could relax and enjoy the rest of my summer.

Everything was going to be okay. I just had to stick to being honest and true to myself and to my friends and family, to sharing my thoughts and feelings, and to getting at the truth without telling stories in my head.

Dreams could come true, but I was in charge of my own destiny.

# Acknowledgments

It takes the perfect mix of ingredients to create a delicious story. I'm very grateful to all the people who were part of the recipe for this book. Super-sized thank-yous to sous-chefs extraordinaire: editor Jenne Abramowitz and agent Tricia Lawrence.

I'm eternally thankful for the children's literature community—writers, artists, educators, readers. In addition to the amazing people I've acknowledged before, I'd like to thank Sarah Darer Littman, Kari Anne Holt, Elise Bryant, Christina Soontornvat, Misa Sugiura, and the #StreetTeam: Winsome Bingham, Kenneth Lewis, Allen Wells, Ebony Mudd, RaQia Lowo, Denise Adusei, and Wiley Blevins for amazing support. For taste-testing my work, thank you to long-time writing partners Kristy Boyce, Andrea Wang, Jo Knowles, and Cindy Faughnan.

I have so much appreciation for the Scholastic team. Thank

you, Stephanie Yang and Jacqueline Li, for the amazing cover, Daniela Escobar, Rachel Feld, Mary Kate Garmire, Nikki Mutch, Abby McAden, Aimee Friedman, Lizette Serrano, Lerina Velazquez, and to copy editor Priscilla Eakeley for preventing me from overseasoning with too many hyphens.

Love and appreciation to my family because I wouldn't be here without them. To my husband, Bob Florence, for cooking amazing meals and eating sushi with me all over the world (Tsukiji market in Tokyo was the best); my daughter, Caitlin Schumacher, for being my favorite eating companion; my stepson, Jason Florence; my mom and stepdad, Yasuko and Bob Fordiani; and my sister and her family, Gail Hirokane, John Parkison, and Laurel Parkison.

# Find more reads you will love . . .

When Jenna Sakai gets dumped, she decides to become totally heartless. No boys. No battles. But keeping her cool isn't easy. Her parents keep fighting about money, her bestie is always busy, and Jenna's ex turns out to be her chief competition for a scholarship she's desperate to win. Luckily, she's got the perfect hiding spot—a diner where she can drown her sorrows in milkshakes after school. Except a cute-but-incredibly-annoying boy keeps stealing her booth . . .

When Maya's family moves to Pennsylvania to open up their pizza shop, Soul Slice, it's a disaster. On Maya's first delivery, she trips and falls face-first into a rude boy's pizza order. Things only get worse when Maya sees the rude—but pretty cute—boy at school. But can surprising friendships and pizza-making lessons turn Maya's new town into her own slice of heaven?

Hedge
Over
Heels

Sometimes the prickliest friends have the biggest hearts.

Elise McMullen-Ciotti

**M**SCHOLASTIC

Rayna may be the new kid at school, but that doesn't mean she wants to make friends! No, the only BFF Rayna wants is a furry, four-legged one. Only instead of the dog she's been dreaming of, Rayna gets a hedgehog named Spike who is as prickly and emo as she is. Will she and her new hedgie hide from a fresh start—and the local pet talent show—or will they take a chance on friendship?

# Have you read all the *wish* books?

☐ *Clementine for Christmas* by Daphne Benedis-Grab

☐ *Snow One Like You* by Natalie Blitt

☐ *Allie, First at Last* by Angela Cervantes

☐ *Gaby, Lost and Found* by Angela Cervantes

☐ *Lety Out Loud* by Angela Cervantes

☐ *Keep It Together, Keiko Carter* by Debbi Michiko Florence

☐ *Just Be Cool, Jenna Sakai* by Debbi Michiko Florence

☐ *Alpaca My Bags* by Jenny Goebel

☐ *Pigture Perfect* by Jenny Goebel

☐ *Sit, Stay, Love* by J. J. Howard

☐ *Pugs and Kisses* by J. J. Howard

☐ *Pugs in a Blanket* by J. J. Howard

☐ *The Love Pug* by J. J. Howard

☐ *Girls Just Wanna Have Pugs* by J. J. Howard

☐ *Best Friend Next Door* by Carolyn Mackler

☐ *11 Birthdays* by Wendy Mass

☐ *Finally* by Wendy Mass

☐ *13 Gifts* by Wendy Mass

☐ *The Last Present* by Wendy Mass

☐ *Graceful* by Wendy Mass

☐ *Twice Upon a Time: Beauty and the Beast, the Only One Who Didn't Run Away* by Wendy Mass

☐ *Twice Upon a Time: Rapunzel, the One with All the Hair* by Wendy Mass

# Read the latest *wish* books!